# DRIP CASTLE

## BRUCE EBERTS

Drip Castle
Copyright © 2019 by Bruce Eberts

Tellwell Talent
www.tellwell.ca

ISBN
978-0-2288-1567-9 (Paperback)
978-0-2288-1568-6 (eBook)

# Acknowledgements

Writing this acknowledgement was probably the hardest part of writing this book. Mainly because I want to thank every person I have ever come in contact with in my life for giving me a dopamine hippocampus memory imprint of life experiences to draw upon to write. As my wife has told me, the accuracy is highly questionable but the imagination is not.

Thank you to the individuals who took my calls at flight schools, gun shops, police stations and fuel companies to add what legitimacy I could to my story. Thank you for not contacting CSIS.

I want to thank Arthur Price, Cam Green, Dave Johannesson, Johnny Hickli and Steve Geddes for allowing me to tell stories after our road hockey games in the northern Ontario town of Cochenour.

We may have been only eleven or twelve years old but it was a delight to lie in the snow, staring up at the stars, and tell them a story. And yes Dave, it was like "Stand By Me."

Thank you to my brother and sisters, my mom, mother-in-law (thanks for the Italian translation!), friends and extended family who had to endure a relentless onslaught of texts, chapter rewrites and verbal character development even when they just asked me the title of the book. Thank you to my late dad for always listening to my dreams, no matter how lofty and the rides to the Griffith Mine when he had to check in on a Saturday as the Superintendent.

Finally, a thank you to my own family.

To my son Tristan who would read the story back to me on our rides back and forth to Laurier University. Thanks for listening and so very proud of all you have done so early in your life.

To my daughter Abigail, whose caring and loving free lance attitude to everyone she encounters, is a lesson to me every day on what is important in life.

And finally to my wife Daiana whose love and support for this book and every other crazy, quirky pursuit I undertake cannot be embellished.

We often joke we are on a fifty year marriage contract after which time we can go our separate ways.

I prefer the option to renew.

for Gary...

ex
libris

Kristen L. Bell

## Chapter One

# TORRISON

"Fuck off, Campbell! You throw any more of that grease-cleaning shit at me, and I'm going to shove it up your ass!" Rick Torrison grabbed a rag off the top of his green work locker and wiped the white cleansing grease from his brown pant leg. "Fucking jerk," he mumbled under the loud laughter of Trent Campbell.

"What's wrong, Torrison? Don't like someone helping you clean up after a shift?" Campbell shouted back.

"What do you know about putting in a shift, Campbell?" Rick said, looking down and continuing to wipe off the grease cleaner. "Last I heard, you cost Rennet Mine fifty grand when you fell asleep on the field crusher and let the belt burn up." Rick took off his work boots and coveralls and placed them back into his locker. He took out his white Adidas runners with the red stripes and his brown leather jacket. He purposely slammed his locker door to try and cut off Trent Campbell's response.

"Didn't fall asleep, and it didn't cost the mine nothing! Fucking belt was worn out. Would have happened on the next shift anyway!"

Trent Campbell was a heavyset, forty-eight-year-old man who had been working at the Rennet Iron Ore Mine since he dropped out of high school. Standing six foot four, he could be intimidating, but his noticeably bulging belly underneath his coveralls made his movements laboured.

A wide strip of bald freckled scalp ran down the centre of his head, bordered on either side by snow white hair. He had a permanently red face, which Rick thought was due to his penchant to yell at people rather than walk over and talk.

Rick sat down on one of the slated work benches between sets of lockers and began tying his shoes. He decided it was worth yelling back at Campbell.

"Yeah, well, I guess the guys who got overtime fixing it aren't complaining." He stood up, put on his leather jacket, and picked up his steel lunch pail. He was about to walk out to catch the mine bus home when Daryl Rykin walked in.

"Don't leave yet, boys!" Rykin yelled. "Time for some shift changes! And don't worry, the buses will wait."

Daryl Rykin was the plant shift foreman. He was tall and so skinny that his coveralls looked like a clown suit. Rick often thought he should be wearing a big red wig and floppy shoes instead of a hard hat and work boots. Rykin didn't like Rennet, he didn't like his job, and he didn't like his workers. But what Rykin did like was to see others in misery. The only time you saw a smile on his face was when you had misery on yours. The workers knew him as "Daryl the Dickhead." He eagerly took on the worst jobs for his crew just so he could see their faces drop when he assigned them.

Rykin gave out papers outlining crew and shift changes to the various men. He handed Rick his and smiled.

Rick Torrison was thirty-three years old. He weighed 160 lbs, had a slim build, and stood five foot eleven (six feet if you asked him personally). His hair was light brown and was close to a buzz cut, which often made him stand out against the longer hairstyles of 1971. He graduated from Tear Falls High School in 1955. The following year, he went to college, but he only lasted a few months before becoming tired of the routine and always being short of money. In 1957, he joined the Canadian army and was sure he had found his true calling. The guys were tough but loyal, and the army actually paid on time. It was enough to keep him there for nearly six years.

Rick took a moment to sit down and study the paper. He raised his head to a voice from across the room.

"You're a fucking dick, Rykin!" someone yelled. Rykin didn't even bother to see who made the comment. He simply turned and walked out of the locker room with a perverse smile of satisfaction. *Daryl the Dickhead*, he said to himself. He liked living up to his name.

Rick looked back at his paper to see he had been moved to the midnight-to-8 a.m. shift, otherwise known as the graveyard shift.

"Shit!" he said under his breath. He was just getting used to his afternoon shift starting at 4 p.m. and ending at midnight. Resigned, he put the paper in the side pocket of his leather jacket and walked out of the locker room to get on a mine bus for the ride home. He made a point of stepping over the legs of a seated Trent Campbell.

"Fuck you, Campbell," he said. It was now 12:15 a.m.

In 1963, Rick had left the army and begun a job at a local seaplane company called Brown Airways. The company had a fleet of float planes and was owned by Pat Galverson. The work and pay were good, but Rick's real reward was getting his training and flight hours for his bush plane pilot's license. By the summer of 1965, Rick was a fully licensed bush pilot flying for Brown Airways.

Everything went well for Rick at Brown Airways. He was promoted a number of times and got along well with his co-workers. Then, in July of 1968, he showed up to work to see everyone standing around outside the main office. One of the other pilots just looked at him and gave him two thumbs down. Brown Airways had gone bankrupt.

Rick walked out into the mine parking lot, where various school- and coach-style buses were lined up to take the afternoon shift home. It was mid-July, but the Northern Ontario night still had most workers wearing light jackets. Rick's hometown of Tear Falls was exactly an hour away. He always felt lucky on the shift ride home, for of all the buses to be on, the best was Manny Prost's coach.

Rick jumped up the stairs of Manny's bus and greeted him with his usual apology. "Sorry for the dirt, Manny."

"That dirt means money, Rick! Not to worry," Manny replied with a grin.

Rick quietly counted the seat rows as he moved to the back of the bus. "Ten, eleven, twelve." He stopped and hopped into his regular window seat of the twelfth row.

"Comfortable, Rick?" Manny yelled back, smiling in the bus's large rear-view mirror.

"Always, Manny," Rick said, smiling back.

Manny Prost had been driving buses for Prost Bus Lines for twenty-five years. He'd started the business after picking up hitchhikers on the road with his father's truck. At the age of fifty-one, Manny had built Prost Bus Lines into a fleet, and his pride and joy was the 1967 MC6 motor coach he drove to the mine. He believed the workers deserved the comfort of its fifty-five plush captain seats and a smooth ride after a long shift. He kept it impeccably clean and could often be seen shining up the silver handrails as he waited for the workers to come off shift.

Rick sat in his seat and stared out the window. He watched as Trent Campbell roared out of the parking lot in his VW camper van. *Shithead can't even bring himself to take the bus like everyone else*, he thought. He turned his attention to the aisle as other workers began filing onto the bus. All were greeted by Manny, and a few wisecracks were thrown around with some loud laughs. It wasn't long before he spotted his friend Milt Tonkin's gleaming smile. Milt jumped into his usual seat beside Rick.

"Uh oh," Milt said. "I see the blank shift stare going on. What is it this time? Got turned down by Jasmine Rubuwen again?"

"Nah, didn't even see her all shift," Rick replied. He stared out the window. "Why is it Campbell wastes all that money on gas when he could take the bus for free?"

"That's what's bothering you?" Milt replied. "Trent Campbell driving his van to the mine?"

"I can do without the psychoanalysis, Freud. Just answer the question. It doesn't make sense. He has always been a cheap bastard, as far as I know."

"Well, if you really want to know, I think it's because the guy stinks. He takes all his clothes home every shift in that large duffle bag he carries. You want him on this bus with that bag?" Milt asked with a smile.

"Guess not." Rick looked back up to the front of the bus and saw Manny was eating an apple. "C'mon, Manny, let's go."

"Okay, it isn't Jasmine, and it ain't Trent Campbell. So, what is it, buddy?" Milt placed his shoulder bag under the seat in front of him. "What's got you so on edge tonight that you can't even let Manny finish his apple?"

Rick reached into the side pocket of his leather jacket, took out the note from Rykin, and handed it to Milt without breaking his gaze.

Milt took the piece of paper and rotated it several times to get the proper light to read it. "Ah, the shift change!" he said upon seeing the initials D.R. at the bottom of the page. "You know you should really get out of the plant and come work in the pit, Rick. We've got Seminsky for shift foreman, and the guy rarely makes it to work, let alone changes people around on shifts."

Rick stopped watching Manny and sat up in his seat to get more comfortable. "No thanks, Milt. You guys eat more dust than I do." He stuck his hand out, and when Milt returned the paper, he continued. "Better yet, how about we trade you Rykin for Seminsky. Then you guys can accidentally run him over with a yuke."

Milt brushed his long black hair back, put on his mine cap, and pulled it down over his eyes for the ride home. "No way... We did that one already. How do you think we got Seminsky? Although..." He sat up again and pushed his hat up. "What we could do is ask Oakey out at the tailings pond to get rid of him. That shit's like quicksand. You would never find him again!" Milt stared at Rick, raising his eyebrows several times to emphasize his point.

Rick was unimpressed and tilted his seat back. "Fucking Oakey," he mused. He turned back to Milt, who was settling himself back into his sleep pose. "Does that fucking guy actually have a last name?"

"I don't know," Milt said, his hat now comfortably pulled down over his face. "In fact, I don't even know if Oakey is his first or last name. It's all he's got on his hard hat. I do believe the guy is crazy enough to do anything. He once came after me with a shovel. Bastard nearly took my head off!"

The conversation was interrupted by Manny closing the bus door and calling back to the workers, "Anyone know if there are any latecomers?" A few muffled noes were enough for Manny to shut down the aisle lights, put the bus into gear, and start driving the three miles of gravel road to the main highway.

Rick watched as the bus went underneath the lighted Rennet Mine sign as they approached the intersection to the highway. To the left was a smaller sign that read "There is safety in numbers! Over 7 months with no lost time accidents!" Rick wondered how this would make the guy who had the accident on the eighth month feel.

The Rennet Mine was named after Robert Rennet, a prospector who discovered the iron ore body at the site in 1960. It wasn't until 1963 that enough government and private money was invested in the operation to get the mine up and running. The product was producing iron ore pellets for the steel mills down south. Most every job at Rennet Mine was unionized, and most every job was well paid.

Manny stopped the bus at the highway junction and took a good look both ways. There was rarely any traffic out on the highway at this hour, but he was always wary of the odd trucker trying to make a deadline and driving fast late at night. Assured it was safe, he pulled out onto Highway 205. The sounds and bright lights of the mine soon faded and were quickly replaced by the darkness of a narrow strip of Northern Ontario highway. The chatter coming from the workers died down, and everyone seemed to accept the fact the hour-long drive home was best spent relaxing or sleeping.

Rick looked over at Milt and could tell he was already fast asleep. He turned back to the window and once again gazed out. He watched the moon flash behind the tall tree tops and listened in a trance as Manny took the coach diesel engine through its gears to bring the bus up to a comfortable highway speed.

Rick couldn't blame Milt for sleeping. It was hard not to sleep on Manny's bus. The coach glided down the highway, absorbing every bump with an ease that sometimes made Rick wonder whether the bus was moving at all. The seats reclined, and Rick was sure Manny had specifically tuned the diesel engine to hum at the frequency used for hypnosis.

But Rick couldn't sleep. He moved and shifted in his seat with little relief. He dreaded the upcoming shift change. He wondered if Trent Campbell would follow him to his new shift, or worse, Daryl Rykin. He worried about his health, and he worried about his mom. Rick never stopped worrying about his mom.

Milt woke up and gave Rick a nudge as the bus slowed down for the first stop at the NearNorth Motel and Bar located on the main highway running through Tear Falls.

"NearNorth!" Manny yelled back to the workers as the hissing air brakes brought the bus to a comfortable stop.

Milt looked over again at Rick, who was still fast asleep. "Wake up, Rick," he said giving his friend a shoulder bump. He reached down to put his cap into his shoulder bag. He sat back up and looked over at Rick, who was stretching, his eyes open. "You know your snoring is not getting any better there, Torrison. Starting to think my mine earplugs could be better used for the ride home."

Milt Tonkin was thirty-one years old and had been Rick's best friend since grade school. He was slightly shorter and thinner than Rick, standing five foot ten and weighing 150 lbs. Rick often thought Milt had the ideal life. He was married to his beautiful wife, Kristen, and they had two healthy boys, five and six years old, to whom Rick had been granted the unofficial title of uncle.

Rick often described Milt as a real "go-getter," but Milt was always quick to correct him and say, "Nope...I'm a go-better." And that was always Milt's philosophy on life. Nothing seemed to get him down. He once broke his arm in a track and field high jump competition, but he only saw it as lucky he didn't break both arms. When his new 1969 green GTO was stolen, he said he would save on gas. When Rick lost his job at Brown Airways, Milt said a better-paying job would come along. It was shortly thereafter that he vouched for Rick and got him a job at Rennet Mine.

Manny let off a group of workers at the motel stop, and Rick watched out the window as they got into their cars or started their walk home. It was now 1:20 a.m. Manny said goodbye and gave a few waves to the exiting workers. Then he closed the door and eased the bus out of the parking lot.

The bus had just hit third gear before it started to slow down again for a stop at the corner of Balsam and Raven Streets. "BR!" Manny yelled out.

Milt and Rick stretched their legs as they waited for the other workers to exit. Milt got out of his seat with Rick right behind. At the end of the aisle, Milt made a point of placing a hand on Manny's shoulder.

"When are you going to get me a nice shirt like this, Manny?" he said.

"As soon as you cut your hair, Tonkin," Manny replied. Milt bounded down the bus stairs with a laugh.

Rick approached Manny next. "Won't be seeing you for a while, Manny. Switching over to the graveyard shift after a few days off." He went down the stairs and turned back to give Manny a salute goodbye.

Manny already had his hand on the bus's chrome lever to close the door, but he paused. He lowered his voice so as to not have his words carry to anyone else left on the bus. "Fucking Rykin?"

"Fucking Rykin," Rick echoed back.

Manny responded with a flat smile and shook his head. His gaze shifted over Rick's shoulder, to Milt's face. "Too bad you couldn't take that guy with you, Rick!" he said. Rick laughed as Manny nodded and closed the coach bus door.

Milt and Rick stood under a street light and watched as Manny's bus drove off with some trailing dust kicked up from the gravel shoulder of the paved street. The other workers were already walking home and quickly faded off into the late summer night. It was now 1:30 a.m.

Milt looked up to the hum of the failing street light illuminating the two men. A familiar swarm of insects could be seen flying around the light post in a spell of false daylight. He turned to Rick. "Where do you think the mine buys its light bulbs? They never seem to burn out."

"I don't know, Milt," Rick replied as the two men started their common walk home.

Even with a swelling population of near 1,800, Tear Falls streets became traditionally quiet and still by this time of night. Few cars were on the streets, and even if one did pass, Rick and Milt would probably know who it was and wonder why they were out so late.

The two men walked for a few minutes without speaking. The silent night allowed the stepping sounds of Rick's shoes and Milt's boots to be clearly distinguishable. A cricket choir from the nearby ditch served as background, and the combination of sounds was strangely meditative for both men. Rick finally turned to his friend and said, "I think I need to pick up more work, Milt."

"Yeah, and do what? Milt replied, kicking a pebble into the ditch and continuing to stare straight ahead. "You going to start your own seaplane business?"

"That would be too easy. I was talking to Paul Rocelli over at the airport. He needs some help with a guy to drive his aviator fuel trucks. Hours are flexible. He is too busy with his own in-town fuel deliveries."

Milt could tell by Rick's voice that he was half serious about the job. He purposely slowed his walk to give them more time to talk before reaching their homes.

"What's Rocelli going to pay you over there? Seven...maybe eight bucks an hour? That's half of what you're making at the mine. Why don't you just work more overtime? And how are you going to fit that in with your mine shifts anyway?"

Rick stopped walking, forcing Milt to do the same. The two men were now between street lights, with a three-quarter moon making up for the lost light.

"Milt, I need the money," Rick said with a measure of both despair and conviction. "My mom's medical bills keep piling up, and the government doesn't help worth shit. Besides, it will get me around planes again."

"What d'ya mean they don't pay. I thought the government paid for everything," Milt replied.

Rick's mother had been coping with multiple sclerosis for over ten years. Rick remembered his dad phoning him in basic training, saying he thought there was something wrong with her. She was starting to have difficulty walking and keeping her balance. At first, his dad thought she might have been drinking too much. But the symptoms got progressively worse until they went to see a specialist from out of town. The diagnosis came back as multiple sclerosis, or MS, as the family came to know health care terminology. Things only got worse when Rick's dad died four years later in a snowmobile accident. His mother now only walked short distances with a walker, and Rick had to borrow a wheelchair for any long trips outside the house.

Rick started walking again. He could now see Milt's home. "Ah, they pay for the doctor appointments and a few drugs, but they don't pay for a lot of the special medicine. And who do you think pays for the help to watch over her or make her a meal when I'm not home? She used to be a workhorse, Milt, and now this!"

"Hey, listen…" Milt said. "If you need some extra money, I think Kristen and I can cough up a few bucks."

"Thanks for the offer. But I want to do this on my own. That's why I want the extra job. I've already chewed through the forty grand my father left us, and it's only been a little over six years since he died. I just hope I have enough money to take her to Mexico again for Christmas. It's the one thing she looks forward to all year."

Milt could detect his friend's frustration, so to lighten the mood, he said, "Yeah that's a great trip you two take! You still stay at that place outside Tijuana…and what's the name of your buddy that owns that place?" Milt asked.

A smile reappeared on Rick's face. "The Larga Vida Villa. Eduardo Samos is the owner. He's a great guy, and I consider him a friend. He always makes sure my mom gets a ground-floor room. He's the one that keeps saying there is a hospital in Tijuana that has special treatment for my mom's MS and he would help out with getting her set up."

The two men had reached Milt's driveway, and once again, they stopped. "Ever thought of taking him up on the offer?" Milt asked delicately, knowing it would cost more money.

"I've thought about it," Rick replied. "I was actually thinking of calling Eduardo to see if he could check into some costs for me. Easier for him to do it than a gringo in broken Spanish."

"Why don't you call him then? You've got nothing to lose."

"Yeah…maybe… I want to see if I get the airport job first."

"Well, think about the extra overtime at the mine. Shit, I could even fuck up the field crusher belt like Campbell did just to give you guys some extra work!"

Rick gave him a smile as he turned and began his own walk home. "You do that, Milt, and say hi to Jasmine Rubuwen for me!"

"I'll do that for me, not you, Torrison!" Milt yelled after him.

The back of Rick's hand went up in a wave as he disappeared into another shadow of the darkened street.

Chapter Two

# LAGO CARBURANTE

R ick sat in Paul Rocelli's Lake Fuels airport office looking around at the pictures on the wall. Most were of Paul and his father, Giovani, posing with celebrities who had flown in for some Northern Ontario hunting or fishing. There were always stories around town that some famous person had flown into Tear Falls on a personal plane, but by the time anyone figured out who it might be, they had vanished as fast as the rumour. Rick could see other pictures were of Paul and his father posing with elected mayors and officials, mostly to do with airport projects.

The door of Paul Rocelli's office flew open, and Paul came hurrying in. He took off his gas-stained work gloves and threw them on his grey steel desk. Rick recoiled as the distinct odour of aviation fuel hit his nose with a punch.

"You Rick?" Paul asked, throwing out his hand for a shake.

"Yeah...Rick Torrison." Rick stood up and shook Paul Rocelli's hand.

Paul was wearing a worn one-piece coverall that Rick imagined at one time had been a bright orange but now passed for almost a dull black with only a smattering of orange still visible. Paul was a large man. Not overweight, just big. He had thick, wavy black hair that was cut around his ears but in desperate need of a combing or maybe some sort of dethatching. Rick watched as Paul sat down and started fumbling with what Rick assumed was his resume.

"You know how to drive one of those trucks out there, Rick?" Paul Rocelli said, now blindly pointing out the office window to one of his parked eight-ton aviation fuel trucks.

Rick followed his finger to make sure they were looking at the same truck. "Yup!" he replied. "Drove the same type of truck carrying water at the mine. I've also got my DZ license if I need to take it on the road. Not a problem."

"Yeah…well, trucking water and trucking flammable plane fuel can be two different things," Paul said. He continued to look down at Rick's resume.

Paul Rocelli had taken over Lake Fuels from his father after he had suffered a stroke three years ago. His father had emigrated from Italy to Tear Falls in 1937, wanting a fresh start for his family. He originally planned to get a well-paying job in one of the gold mines but he ended up driving an oil delivery truck for a company from out of town. After almost ten years, he figured he could do the job better and make more money if he started his own local fuel delivery business. He used savings, and with help from family and his close Italian friends, he opened up Lake Fuels at the Tear Falls airport in 1949. It was in 1967, at the age of sixty-one, that Giovani suffered a stroke and eventually decided to turn over the business to his eldest son, Paul.

Paul looked farther down Rick's resume. "See here you have your bush pilots licence."

"Yeah, I used to fly for Brown Airways. Did a lot of tourist camp runs, reserve fly-ins, government shit."

Paul looked up. "Wasn't that owned by Pat Galverson?"

"Yup. Good guy with some bad luck!"

"Yeah. How so?"

"I don't know. He had a big heart, but he wasn't much of businessman. He signed our paycheques, but he always said he had to talk to his investors whenever he had to make a decision."

Paul looked back down to Rick's resume. "I think those investors were the bank, Rick. The guy stiffed our family for fifteen grand in fuel before he went bankrupt and took off up north."

Rick nodded in silence, sensing it was a topic best not discussed at the time of an interview.

Paul put Rick's resume down and leaned back in his oak spring chair. A distinct crack could be heard as the chair strained. "You're still working at the mine, Rick?"

"Yeah."

There was an awkward silence as Paul nonchalantly secured his hands behind his head and rocked in his chair. Rick was unsure of who should be taking the lead in the conversation, so he nervously sat up and locked his hands together while resting his elbows on the arms of his own chair.

Paul Rocelli sat forward and placed his hands on the desk. "I guess I don't get it, Rick. Why would you want to come here and give up your weekends and evenings to work for half of what you can get at the mine?"

"Yeah, I know," Rick said. "It seems weird, doesn't it. Even my friends say I should just work more overtime, but there is only so much of the mine a guy can take. And I wouldn't mind being around planes again and maybe even seeing the odd famous person." He nodded at the pictures on Paul's office wall.

Paul got up from his chair and walked over to a bank of wooden drawers underneath a counter that lined one of his office windows. He pulled open a drawer, took out a piece of paper, and then opened a second and took out another. He brought the papers back to his desk and sat down.

"Here," he said as he slid the two pieces of paper over to Rick. "The one piece of paper tells you about the job. What you can do and what you can't screw up. The second is your application. All the stuff we need to know to pay you." Paul sat back for a moment to let Rick glance over the writing. "Pay is seven fifty an hour. Mostly weekend and evening shifts. If you can't do a shift, I call someone else. Don't care about bullshit excuses!"

Rick looked up with the realization that Paul had just offered him the job on the spot. "Sounds good." He stood up and shook Paul's hand. "And when would I start...?" he asked reluctantly, thinking he was already pushing his luck.

"I'll call you. Go home and read that stuff over. See whether you still want the job." Paul picked his gloves up off the desk as a signal to Rick that the interview was over and he had to get back to work.

Rick walked out the door as Paul followed close behind. He looked over to one of the Lake Fuels trucks and turned around as Paul was about to walk away. "Hey, Paul, how did your dad ever come up with the name Lake Fuels? Doesn't sound very Italian to me. Any story behind that?"

Paul broke out in a smile and walked back over to Rick. He took off one glove and cupped Rick's chin in his hand while he put his other arm around his shoulder. "E cosi che possiamo soddisfare questi mangia cake," he said. He then walked away with an even bigger smile than before.

Chapter Three

# BARS IN PLANE SIGHT

ilt walked into the NearNorth Motel bar to the sound of cracking pool balls, the jukebox, and the usual laugh track of a drinking crowd. He was wearing his Friday night bar attire: a white t-shirt, denim jacket and jeans, and a Brown Airways hat that Rick had given him. He took a moment to scan the seats and tables for Rick. It was 8 p.m., and the place was already busy with the summer seasonal workers and the locals mixing in a game of cat and mouse pick-up. The bar was dimly lit, and there was enough simmering cigarette smoke to make it difficult for him to find Rick by looking around. He turned his shoulders sideways and pushed through the crowd. A few guys from work yelled out his name as he navigated the crowded tables, but he ignored them. He finally spotted Rick sitting in one of the red velour booths that lined the back walls of the bar. He could see he was wearing his familiar brown leather jacket and was looking up and talking to the motel's owner, Roddy Simone.

"Hey, Rod," Milt said as he gave him a pat on the back and slipped around him into the booth seat opposite Rick.

"Hi, Milt," Roddy said.

Rick gave Milt a brief look so as to not interrupt Roddy Simone's train of thought.

Roddy Simone, forty years old, had owned the NearNorth Motel for over ten years. He was six foot five, with a physique and build that had people assuming he was a professional bodybuilder or a pro football player who was a long way from home. In reality, his fitness was a product of just being a picky eater and having a set of barbells and a chin-up bar in his motel office. Roddy had moved to Tear Falls with his family when he was fourteen. His dad was a dentist from overseas, and the town had rolled out the red carpet for him to set up his practice. Roddy and his family were also black, something that was not lost on anybody in the town of Tear Falls, which was ninety-five percent white.

Milt sat quietly, listening in on Roddy and Rick's conversation.

"Not sure what your mom can do about the pain, Rick," Roddy said. "I'll ask my dad, but all a dentist knows is how to stop the pain in your mouth."

"Thanks, Roddy," Rick replied. "It's been a tough go lately. Sometimes she wakes up in the middle of the night with these cramps in her legs. She screams like someone's killing her. Freaks me out, and all I can do is stretch her legs, but it doesn't help much."

"And what about all this medical equipment you said your mom might need? Hospital bed, wheelchair stuff?"

"Nope. Government pays only the basics, but ask for anything extra that can actually help, and they tell you to fuck off. Even the drugs the specialist recommends are not covered by Rennet or the government. That's why I'm going to pick up the extra work at the airport driving one of Rocelli's fuel trucks."

A few drum rolls and a mic check from an out-of-town band had all three men turning their heads.

Milt used the distraction to join the conversation. "This band any good, Rod?" he asked.

"Don't know... First time I've heard them," Roddy said. He turned back to Milt and Rick. "But all bands sound good with enough beers...right, boys! I'll send Tracy right over!"

He turned and made his way back in the direction of the bar.

Milt said to Rick, "Couldn't have ordered me a beer, could you? Ya cheap bastard."

"Yeah, well, I didn't know if Kristen was going to let you out, Milton," Rick replied, smiling and slowly sipping his own beer. His attention turned to someone across the room. "Hey, isn't that Jasmine Rubuwen over there at the end of the bar?"

Milt stood halfway up in the booth to take a look. "Yeah, that's her. Damn, that's one fine ass on that woman," he said with outstretched neck.

"Kristen know you talk about Jasmine Rubuwen's ass that way?" Rick said as Milt sat back down.

"What'd you mean? Kristen says the same thing about her ass." Milt flashed Rick a big smile.

"You're a degenerate, Tonkin."

Tracy made her way over to their booth and took out her book to take the men's drink order. "What'll it be, guys?"

"Give us two Blues, Tracy," Rick said.

"Just two, Rick?" Tracy asked. "Won't be making it back over here again until after the band finishes its first set. You'll have to do better than that."

"Alright...make it two rye and the two Blues as chasers," Rick said with a smile

"Two Blues and two rye," Tracy repeated as she made a note on her flip pad and headed over to another table.

Milt looked back at Rick. "Well... tell me what happened with Rocelli? He hired you already? He must be a desperate man!"

"Yeah...well, desperate or not, I start training next Saturday," Rick said. "Looking forward to it."

"I was talking to my brother about Paul Rocelli. He went to school with him." Milt was already scanning for Tracy's return. "Says he's a good guy. His dad can be an asshole, but I heard he got sick or something so he's not around much."

"I didn't see his dad other than in some of the pictures on the wall, so couldn't tell ya." Rick noticed Milt was now staring past his side of the booth, towards the door.

"Well, here comes trouble," Milt said.

Rick moved over in the booth and looked in the same direction. "That the DeMello twins?" he asked.

"Looks like it," said Milt as he lost the twins walking through the crowd and towards the bar. "Roddy's not going to like that!"

"Ah…maybe they have grown up," Rick said, raising his eyebrows.

Tracy interrupted the men as she came back to the table with their drinks. "What's got you men's attention so much over there?" She asked as she placed her tray down and set a shot of rye and beer in front of each man. "You're not still chasing Jasmine, are you Rick?" She leaned on the table and looked straight at him.

Rick had known Tracy Rellis all his life. They weren't close friends, but both had grown up in Tear Falls together, first going to elementary school and then graduating high school in the same class. Tracy was tall and slim but was best known for her trademark glowing red hair, which she always wore in a long braid down her back. While Rick and most of his class had gone off to college, Tracy had stayed in town and married her high school sweetheart. When her husband died of cancer three years later, Tracy took Roddy up on an offer to work the front desk of the NearNorth Motel. She took the weekend bar work as a way to show Roddy her appreciation and to pick up the extra tip money to provide for her young son.

"I'm not—"

"Sure, he's chasing her!" Milt blurted out.

"Thanks, Milt," Rick said. He reached into his wallet, took out a five-dollar bill, and gave it to Tracy to end the conversation.

She walked away, looking back at Rick with a coquettish smile.

"Man, you should ask her out," Milt said, tracking Tracy's walk towards the bar.

"I have enough problems." Rick took a drink of his beer.

"I don't know if that would be much of a problem," Milt replied, still staring in Tracy's direction. The men's attention was broken by the band kicking in with a cover version of The Guess Who's "American Woman."

Rick and Milt raised their shot glasses of rye for a toast. "To your mom and many more Mexico trips!" Milt yelled over the music.

"And to you never getting Dickhead Rykin as a shift foreman," Rick replied. "Bottoms up!"

The men followed their shots of rye with a healthy chug of beer and then sat back in the booth with their backs against the wall, facing out, listening to the band. Both men were careful to keep their feet off the red velour seats as a measure of respect for Roddy.

The band was starting its third song when Rick spotted the DeMello twins headed their way. "Ah, fuck, Milt…here they come. They're looking for a place to sit!"

Milt looked over and could see Marty and David DeMello walking slowly through the packed bar, looking for seats. Marty was wearing a powder blue jean vest over a white t-shirt, while David had on a tight red t-shirt with white stripes around the shoulders and a white number seven on the front. Both men were wearing jeans and had worn running shoes on their feet. The two twins both measured about five foot ten, had thick necks, and were extremely stocky. It was hard to knock them over in hockey, football, or any activity for that matter. Although they were identical, Marty possessed a small scar on his chin from a childhood playground accident. It was what Rick, Milt, and most people in Tear Falls used to tell the two twins apart.

Milt watched their progress closely and thought they might have evaded the twins' attention when he saw David grab an empty chair. But his brother overruled him upon seeing the extra room in Milt and Rick's booth and motioned to his brother to head in their direction. The two twins were soon on their way over, both with a beer in each of their hands.

"Hey, boys!" Marty said. "Thanks for saving us some seats!"

Milt and Rick both sat up, knowing there was not much choice but to let the brothers in.

Marty and David DeMello were three years older than Rick. They worked at their father's sawmill and came from a family of six boys. All the DeMello boys seemed to have been born tough, but Rick thought this was more out of necessity than design. Their mother and father were rarely home due to running the business, and the sons were encouraged to solve their own problems by whatever means were available. This was especially true of the twins. Marty and David both played hockey and were known for having some of the hardest slap shots in the local hockey leagues. But what the twins really liked to do was fight. Both on and off the ice, the twins never backed down from a confrontation no matter how the odds were stacked.

Marty and David sat down, and speaking loudly over the music, Marty said, "Your boys going to play hockey again this year, Tonkin?"

"Yeah, they'll be in Novice this year," Milt replied.

"Good...I think they may be playing with my boy, Chad," Marty said. "He can show them how to take a slap shot!" he added with a grin. Marty turned his attention to Rick. "And what about you, army man? Still at Rennet?"

"Unfortunately, yes," Rick said, taking a drink.

Both Rick and Milt were purposely keeping their responses short, hoping the twins would tire of their company and quickly find seats elsewhere.

David took his turn to question Rick. "I heard Rocelli hired you to drive one of his fuel trucks. Why you helping out that old wop anyway? He should get his sons off their asses to help him."

"It was his son Paul who hired me," Rick replied. "Just want the extra money to take care of my mom and take her on a trip to Mexico."

"Oh yeah...she's got the cancer, right..." Marty chimed in.

"Nope...MS...multiple sclerosis."

David leaned on the table with his thick forearms crossed and looked directly at Rick. "You should come and work at our sawmill, Torrison. Our old man would pay you double what Rocelli would pay. We start at ten bucks an hour and go up from there."

From the look on Rick's face, Milt could tell he was actually going to respond to David's offer.

"How would I—"

"Rick wants to be around the planes and shit," Milt said, cutting Rick off. "He has his bush pilot's license. Never know, someone might pick him up for a job flying." He looked anxiously at Rick over his beer as he took a drink.

Rick squinted as he stared back at Milt, but he said nothing.

"Whatever," David replied, sitting back. "Just trying to help out a fellow citizen in need of money." He laughed and toasted his brother.

Marty turned back to Rick. "So, if you need extra money, why don't you just take a few bars of gold off the Stinson gold plane when you fill it up. Imagine that would pay for a few trips to Mexico."

"Sure, why not!" Rick joked. "I could even give some bars out to the family. When does this plane come in? Once a year for Christmas?"

"No, stupid!" Marty said. "They have a plane that transports the gold bars they pour at their mine. Happens all the time. Man…you're dense, Torrison!"

Rick didn't have a chance to respond as David hit Marty on the arm. "Nobody gives a shit about a stupid plane," David said. He looked back out to the bar crowd. "These guys are losers. Let's go back to the bar and talk with Tracy. I need some more beer anyway."

"Sure," Marty said. "Maybe we can even get you a date with Jasmine Rubuwen." The twins stood up, guzzled their beers, and left the empties on the table before heading over to the bar.

Milt turned to Rick. "You know, it's not worth getting into a conversation with those assholes. And a job at the DeMello sawmill? Probably wind up sawed up like the logs."

Rick ignored his comment. "What's Marty talking about with this Stinson gold plane? The Stinson Mine has a plane?"

"Well, they must have one or rent one. How else do you think they get the gold out?" Milt replied. He was now stretching his legs out and once again leaning his back against the end of the booth.

"Not sure," Rick said following Milt's lead to stretch out. "Guess I've never thought about how they get the gold out. Never seen their plane at the airport before."

"You really think they are going to advertise it?" Milt said, turning to Rick. "Hey, everyone! Look over here. Here's the plane with all the gold in it!"

Rick laughed. "Yeah, I guess not." He decided to change the subject for the sake of saving himself some embarrassment. "Hey, I think we need more beer and more rye!"

Milt agreed and started a full arm wave to Tracy across the room.

Rick and Milt spent the rest of the night drinking, laughing, and occasionally singing along with the band. They talked about Rick's new job and why Trent Campbell hadn't been fired at the mine, and they speculated on why someone as good looking as Jasmine Rubuwen was still single at twenty-nine. But throughout the night, Rick was still thinking about what Marty DeMello had said about the Stinson Gold Mine plane. He wondered whether he might actually be filling up a plane and just happen to look in the window and see a stack of shiny gold bars. He was fascinated by the thought.

It was now 12:15 a.m., and the band finished off their night as they'd begun, playing the song "American Woman."

Milt looked over at Rick with glassy eyes. His jean jacket was on the floor of the booth, and his hat was providing cover for a collection of empty beer bottles on the table. "Didn't they just play this song?" he asked, showing obvious signs of inebriation.

"Yeah, like three hours ago," Rick said with a laugh. "Think it might be best we start the walk home, Tonks."

Roddy Simone was already making the rounds to the different tables to announce last call, and eventually he made it over to Rick and Milt's booth. He slid in beside Milt, a white bar towel slung over his blue plaid bush shirt.

"Looks like you guys did some damage tonight," he said as he moved the empty beer bottles and rye glasses, arranging them at the end of the table.

"We did our fair share," Rick said with a smile.

"By the looks of Tonkin here, I would say more than your fair share." Roddy placed a hand on Milt's shoulder and gave him a shake. "You okay, buddy?"

"Yup, time to go home," Milt said, struggling to respond.

Roddy grinned at Milt and stood up from the booth. He motioned over to Tracy for a pickup of the glasses and beer bottles.

He turned back to Rick and Milt. "Well, you boys…" He didn't finish his sentence. A commotion had started across the room. "Just a sec, guys… Be back."

He strode through the bar crowd, shoving people aside to get to the disturbance. There he found both of the DeMello twins delivering and taking blows from what appeared to be at least six other men. Roddy grabbed Marty DeMello around the neck and pulled him back out of the fray, yelling in his ear, "Don't you have a wife and kid at home, DeMello! Don't want to wind up in jail or worse, now, do you!"

He threw Marty down into an open booth and went back to get his brother. He grabbed a man off David DeMello's back at the same time David was kneeling and trading punches with another man on the floor. Roddy firmly grabbed David's arm, pulled him up, and pushed him toward his brother.

"Time for you guys to go!" he yelled. "Now!"

Marty looked up, holding his right hand, which was already swollen from a flurry of punches. His white t-shirt under his vest was ripped at the collar, and blood was running on his left arm from a glass cut. "Wanted to take it outside, Roddy. It's those fucking tree-huggers who didn't mind messing your place up!"

David was in no better shape with a swollen left temple, cut lip, and blood on a torn shirt. "You gonna throw those losers out, too, Simone," he said, "or is it just the DeMellos you always want to see in jail?"

"They're going, too. Don't you worry," Roddy said.

David looked over at his brother. "Let's go!"

"Good idea!" Roddy said. "I'll be sending you both a bill in the mail!"

Laughing, the DeMello twins gave a brief glance at the group of men they had just fought and left.

Roddy walked over to the other table of men involved in the fight and asked them to leave. It was not long before things got back to normal, and he resumed informing people about last call.

Rick turned his attention back to Milt. He could see his friend still needed a few minutes to orient himself, so he decided to take the time to walk over to the bar and say goodnight to Roddy. "Be right back, Milt. Just going to say goodnight to Roddy, and then we'll go."

Milt was sitting up with his head tilted back against the booth with his eyes closed. "Take your time."

Rick walked over and into an open space at one end of the bar. He yelled down to Roddy, who was now washing glasses at the other end. "See ya later, Roddy! Thanks for trying to help!"

Roddy made a point of coming down to where Rick was standing and shook his hand. "Sorry about that shit, Rick. Should have known better than to have the DeMellos here."

"Yeah...but I would say you handled it pretty good, Roddy. You have a way. They listen to you. What was that all about anyway?" Rick asked.

"Usual," Roddy said. "Group of out of town tree-planters… too many drinks…Jasmine. You get the idea."

Rick looked down and shook his head with a smile. "Yup… that'll do it." He looked over at Milt. "Well, I gotta go. Have to get my partner over there back safe and sound to his wife."

Roddy could see Milt was now in the process of struggling to get out of the booth and pick up his jean jacket off the floor. "Yeah…you do that, Rick," he said with a smile. He turned back to Rick. "And hey, I'll ask my dad tomorrow about anything he might be able to do for your mom. I don't know, maybe he can get drugs wholesale or something. I'll give you a call!"

"Thanks, Rod! Appreciate it!"

Chapter Four

# IT'S MUTUAL

Rick sat in Paul Rocelli's office and let out a big yawn. He had just finished well over a week of midnight shifts at Rennet Mine, and as he had anticipated, he wasn't sleeping very well. He had flipped briefly through the manual Paul Rocelli had given him at the interview but had come to the conclusion that anything important would be learned on the job.

Impatient, he got up from his chair, walked over to the window, and looked out onto the airport tarmac.

Tear Falls Airport was a typical small Northern Ontario airport. The main terminal building was a one-storey structure that was not much bigger than a large town hall. There was one double-door entrance in and one double-door exit out to board flights. A single ticket counter served the function of verifying tickets, providing security, and accepting checked baggage. Most everyone knew the people who worked at the airport, and it was with some amusement that travellers would often say as many goodbyes to the workers as they would to the people seeing them off.

Other small planes parked at the airport were used by the mining industry, government, and, of course, the odd fly-in tourist who might or might not be famous.

Rick was specifically looking at a group of Cessna planes parked at the far end of the airport, and he wondered whether one of these planes was sitting there full of gold. He'd broken out in a smile at the memory of Milt's comment at the bar just as Paul Rocelli opened the office door.

"See something amusing out there, Rick?" Paul asked, as he motioned to the chair in front of his desk for Rick to sit down.

"No, I was just thinking about a joke a friend told me from work," Rick said. He was quick to direct the conversation back to his new job. "Read the manual as best I could. Pretty straightforward. Need to ask you a few questions about the truck's gas meters and stuff, but I thought some hands-on today would clear that up."

"Good," Paul said, now sitting at his desk and looking down at paperwork. He began filling in some numbers on sheets of paper without saying anything more. Rick did not interrupt and waited patiently for him to finish.

Paul had on his familiar stained-orange coveralls from the interview, while on his head, he now wore a white hat with Lake Fuels written across it in red. The letters F and L were written in Italic to stand out. Looking out the window, Rick could see the lettering and colouring carried over onto all of the Lake Fuels trucks.

Paul abruptly set the paperwork aside, got up, and walked over to a blue double-door steel cabinet. He opened the door, fingered through some orange coveralls, and then threw one over to Rick. "Here, take these, unless you want to buy your own for your next shift. Don't worry, they may be used, but they have all been washed and dry-cleaned. They don't have to fit exact as long as they do the job of saving anything you wear to work. You have to be wearing these at all times you are out on the tarmac. Lets others know you are an airport worker."

"Thanks," Rick said. He put the coveralls on and then replaced his Adidas runners with the mine work boots he had been carrying with him. By the time he finished tying his boots, Paul had put a new pair of work gloves, a new hat, and a Lake Fuels ID card in front of him on the desk.

"The first set of everything is yours. After that, you replace it at your own cost," Paul said. "Place the ID card in your wallet. Likely never need it, but sometimes you get a picky pilot who wants to see it."

Rick looked at the ID card, which was not much more than his name printed by Paul in between the titles "Lake Fuels" and "Tear Falls Airport." He placed it in his wallet, thinking it would probably never serve anything better than being a souvenir.

Paul sat down and brought out a large folded piece of paper from his desk. He turned it around and showed it to Rick. "Here are the flight schedules for all the planes that are due in this week." He pointed to various squares with flight numbers. "Most of them, you'll get to know, along with the pilots. Others may be one-offs where they may make a special request for fuel."

He got up, walked over, and pinned the paper on a bulletin board near the door. "Anything extra someone needs to know for the next shift, you can pin a note on this board beside the schedule." He motioned for Rick to follow him out the door. "C'mon, let's go take a ride in one of the trucks."

The rest of the day, Paul took Rick through the operational and safety procedures of driving the fuel truck and filling up the different planes. They went through the various types of fuel: avgas, mogas, and jet fuel. He showed Rick how to record the billings and payments and what to do in case of emergencies.

On breaks and lunch, Paul told stories of some of the celebrities and high rollers that had come through the airport, how his dad had started the business, and some funny moments on the job. Rick waited for a story about the Stinson Mine gold plane, but Paul never mentioned it.

Three days of training later, Paul Rocelli said he now felt comfortable with Rick taking on his own shifts. The two men got along well, which Rick thought was evidenced by Paul softening his interview ultimatum of either take it or leave it on shifts. Rick was feeling good about the job. He liked being around planes again, and he liked the thought of having the extra money he needed to take his mom to Mexico. He was even thinking he might have enough money to consider the clinic Eduardo had mentioned for treatment of his mom's MS in Tijuana.

Rick arrived home from his airport shift and was greeted by his mother's hired help. She let him know his mother had already eaten dinner and had gone back to bed. She said there was a message by the phone in the living room and an extra plate was set out for him for his own dinner. Rick thanked her and headed to the living room to read the note. He picked up the phone and dialled the number for the NearNorth.

"NearNorth," Tracy answered.

"Oh, hi, Tracy. It's Rick. Is Roddy in? He left me a message to call."

"I'll check, Rick. One minute."

Rick could hear Tracy's muffled voice calling out to Roddy. She placed the phone back to her ear.

"Rick, he is just in a meeting with a sales guy, but he wanted to know if you have time to stop by for a coffee tomorrow morning. He says it's good news."

"Hey, I'm always ready for good news, Tracy. I start later at the mine now. I'll be there around ten. Thanks, Tracy!"

"My pleasure, Rick. See you then!"

Rick walked into the NearNorth at 10 a.m. and looked around to see a few people eating a late breakfast. Most of the tables had been switched around from the evening bar configuration of joining tables together to individual eating tables with four chairs. Rick walked over to the empty bar and sat in a chair. He'd just turned around to gaze at the empty room when he felt a tap on his shoulder. He turned his stool to see Tracy smiling at him.

"A lot quieter this time of day, isn't it," she said. "No fights."

"Yeah," Rick said, taking another look around at the restaurant. "Roddy doing alright, Tracy? I mean, with the business? There's not many people in here."

"Oh yeah, he is doing fine. I know it doesn't look very busy, but Roddy says he makes ends meet. He's hoping for some Christmas parties to be booked this year. Do you want me to get you a coffee before he comes out?"

"That would be great, Tracy."

Rick looked over the liquor bottles behind the bar as Tracy left to get his coffee. He could see Hennessy Cognac, Crown Royal, and a few other labels he didn't even recognize. *Who would know enough to ask for some of this expensive liquor in Tear Falls?* he thought. *Better yet, who can afford to drink it?*

Tracy came back with a coffee for Rick and one for herself and came around and sat with him at the bar.

"I told Roddy you were here. He will be out in a minute," she said. She laid her hand over his. "Now, how is your mother?"

"She is doing as best as can be expected," Rick said, staring down at Tracy's hand on his. "We take it day by day. Just hoping she will be up for our Christmas Mexico trip."

"Well, if I know you, Rick, you will make it happen!"

Rick saw her gaze shift past him down the bar. "Oh, hi, Roddy!" she said. "Look who's here."

Rick glanced over his shoulder to see Roddy. "Hi, Rick. Didn't know you were here yet."

Rick briefly turned back to look at Tracy, but she had already left her seat and was headed over to wait on a table.

Roddy reached out and shook Rick's hand across the bar. "I'll join you at the booth at the back, Rick. Let me get my coffee."

Rick took his coffee and walked across the room to the booth, still trying to make eye contact with Tracy, but she conveniently avoided his stare. Roddy came over with his coffee and joined him.

"I think I may be able to help you with some of this expensive medical equipment you need for your mom. And I have since found out you are not kidding about the price!" Roddy said.

"Hey, I'm all ears, Roddy. Thanks!"

"We have these sales guys that are always trying to sell us new stuff for the motel, including beds," Roddy said. "So, I just happen to suggest to this one guy, how about a hospital bed or a wheelchair? I gave him this story that we were going to make one room available for people that needed that kind of thing who may be visiting the hospital from out of town or something."

"Sounds good, Roddy, but how does that help me? Still costs, doesn't it?" Rick asked.

"Wholesale, my friend!" Roddy replied. "I can get it for half of what you would have to pay, and I write it off under my motel inventory. You just pay me a little bit each month in cash. Human mutual symbiosis, as my dad would say!"

Rick took a sip of his coffee. "This all legal, Roddy? Whatever fancy name you want to call it. The last thing I want to do is get you in trouble."

"I'll be honest, Rick, it's a shortcut. But businesses do it all the time. You need to bend the rules a bit to keep your job, to survive."

Rick looked around the near-empty restaurant and nodded. He was about to reply when he saw Sergeant McIntyre of the Tear Falls police detachment enter the restaurant.

"Uh…think you have company, Roddy," he said, pointing over to the sergeant, who was standing with his hands on his hips and surveying the room.

"I'll be right back, Rick. Give me a minute."

Roddy went behind the bar and waved the sergeant over.

Sergeant McIntyre had been Tear Falls Ontario Provincial Police detachment commander for as long as Rick could remember. He was tall and big boned and matched Roddy in stature. Rick estimated he was at least sixty years old from the closely cut snow white hair residing under his cap. But he also remembered he had been thinking this from the first time he'd laid eyes on the sergeant twenty-five years ago.

Rick could see McIntyre shaking hands with Roddy and sitting down at the bar with a smile. Roddy stepped over to Tracy, who was already coming out of the kitchen with a coffee, and took it from her. He set the coffee in front of the sergeant on the bar.

Rick was relieved to see the two men laughing and seemingly getting along. A few minutes later, the sergeant stood up from his stool and straightened his belt. He pointed to the liquor display on the back wall, and Roddy turned around and took down a bottle of Hennessy. He reached below the bar, placed it in a bag, and gave it to Sergeant McIntyre. The sergeant gave Roddy a smile, shook his hand, and headed out the door.

Roddy put another bottle back to replace the Hennessy and came back to the booth. "Okay, Rick, where were we? What do you say about my idea to help your mom? Want me to get a price?"

Rick was still watching Sergeant McIntyre through the restaurant window as he got into his patrol car with the bag.

He turned back to Roddy. "Everything okay, Roddy? I guess it's probably none of my business, but did you just give Sergeant McIntyre a bottle of Hennessy?"

"Ah, don't worry about that, Rick. Now, I think I can get the bed for about… Rick? Are you paying attention?" Roddy asked, seeing Rick still looking out the window as the cruiser drove away.

"Yeah…I'm paying attention…"

Roddy knew he couldn't continue. He sat back in the booth and let out a sigh. "Rick, we all have skeletons in our closet. Just some people's bones rattle louder than others. McIntyre is a good man, a good cop. He just has some things on the go like the rest of us."

Rick was already feeling bad for thinking the worst of Roddy. He turned his attention back from the window. "Okay, but why come here, Roddy, for your help? Why wouldn't McIntyre just go to the liquor store? Isn't it a bit risky for him and you?"

"Small town, Rick. You know better. Go into the liquor store here and there, and you're okay. Go twice a week and you're the detachment commander, well, that gets people talking."

Roddy sat up to take another drink of his coffee. "But before you go thinking it's all about me being a good Samaritan, I want you to take look around this empty restaurant. It's hard enough to run a restaurant in this town, let alone do it as a black guy."

"I don't get it, Roddy. I don't think most people give a shit in this town that you're black. Just that you serve good food and bring in a decent band once in a while."

"Most don't. You're right. But some do. Parking, liquor licenses, they don't always come easy."

"So, the odd bottle to McIntyre keeps him out of your business?"

"Opposite. Keeps him in my business. Like I said, McIntyre is one of the good ones." Roddy leaned over the table. "Do you really think a black guy could be grabbing some white guys around the neck and throw them out of his bar like I did with the DeMellos and not hear about it?" He sat back and tapped his finished coffee cup as he looked around his empty restaurant. "Nope, McIntyre may have his problems, but he's fair. Don't mind helping him out with his challenges on the job."

"Human mutual…"

"Symbiosis…" Roddy said, looking back at Rick. "Couldn't have said it better myself."

Rick gave Roddy the go-ahead to look into the hospital bed for his mom and left the restaurant. He drove home to go get ready for his mine shift, but he couldn't help but think of McIntyre. How many other people in Tear Falls did he have a mutual symbiosis with to help him with the challenges of his job?

## Chapter Five

# HOT WATER

Rick sat in the mine locker room, waiting for the foreman to come in and brief the men on their jobs for the shift. Many of the workers had set duties for the operation of a particular piece of machinery or department, but Rick was a general labourer. He could be assigned to a different job anywhere on any shift. But trying to take Milt's positive approach, he saw good news in not seeing Daryl Rykin or Trent Campbell on his crew. He had also survived his rotation through the midnight shifts and was glad to be back on afternoons.

Blake Thomas, the shift foreman, entered the room, carrying a pen and clipboard. He began flipping through some papers and started briefing the crew on the shift ahead. He let Rick and two other general labourers know they were assigned to ore pellet clean-up around furnace three. The briefing complete, everyone put on their hard hats and safety glasses and headed out into the plant.

On the way out, Thomas grabbed Rick's arm. "Torrison...you want to do a double shift tonight?"

Rick was about to say no, but then he remembered Milt's words on overtime. "For...?" he asked.

"They need some help over in the truck maintenance bay to steam clean the yukes for painting. Shareholders will be in at the end of September, so everything has to look good."

Rick gave it a quick thought and weighed leaving his mother alone until morning vs the extra money. He decided the money was too good to pass up and that he would give his mother a call at break. "Sure, why not. Put me down," he said.

Blake Thomas started making a note on his clipboard. "Alright, make your way over there next shift. You'll have at least one other guy helping you." His attention turned to another worker, and Rick made his way out the door to head to furnace three.

At the end of the afternoon shift, Rick decided to wash up and grab some snacks at the mine cafeteria. He ducked into a hallway washroom and headed to one of the sinks. The washroom was predictably empty between shifts, so he took his time to take off his watch and hard hat and wash his face. His head turned as another person entered the washroom. He looked over to see a man stop and stare at him with a blank look. The man smiled.

"Hey, Steve, what are you doing in my private washroom so late at night?" he said as he walked over to Rick.

"It's Rick, not Steve, buddy," Rick replied, shaking his hands dry as he turned around.

"Yeah, sorry there, Rick. My name is Dom Santtini. I'm terrible with names. What are you doing in here? Little out of the way for a shift worker to be using this paper-pusher washroom."

Rick delayed his reply. He wasn't bothered by the simple question; he was bothered by the demeanour of the person asking. Santtini was standing tensely, and he was holding an orange mine garbage bag, which, judging by the tightness of his grip, contained something heavy.

"You work in the mine parts department, right?" Rick asked, still eyeing the bag.

"Yeah, I just come in here to take a shit in private after standing around filling part orders all night."

Rick picked up his hard hat and walked by Santtini. "Well, don't let me stand in your way. Good thing I came in before you."

Santtini laughed as Rick exited the washroom. Rick walked down the hallway and turned a corner, and then he heard footsteps near the washroom door. He leaned his head around the corner and looked down the hallway to see Trent Campbell entering the washroom, his large duffle bag slung over his back.

"Wait until he gets a whiff of that!" Rick said with a laugh as he turned to continue his walk. He looked at his watch to judge his time for the start of his next shift and stopped. "Ah shit," he said as he realized he'd left his watch on the washroom sink. He turned back down the hallway and headed for the washroom.

He pushed open the washroom door hard enough for it to hit the back wall with a bang.

"Hey, Santtini! Is it safe to come in here!" he said, letting out a laugh. He walked into the main washroom area, fully expecting to come face to face with Campbell, but it was empty. He looked at the stall doorways for Santtini's feet but saw nothing. He walked over, picked up his watch, and placed it on his wrist. He looked around the washroom in bewilderment, wondering how he could have missed the two men. His eyes were immediately drawn to the washroom waste receptacle. He walked over and slowly tugged on a thumb-sized piece of orange plastic sticking out of the lid. He drew out a large orange garbage bag. "What the hell?" he said, holding up the bag and examining it. His attention was diverted by the sound of the washroom door opening and the sight of a mine foreman walking in.

"Oh, sorry," the foreman said. "This washroom on clean-up?"

"Uh…no… I was… Actually, yeah… I was just finishing up." Rick pushed the mine garbage bag back into the receptacle. "All yours!" He exited the washroom and walked down the hallway. *What the fuck…? Fucking Campbell*, he thought. He looked down at his watch and broke into a trot.

Rick arrived at the large maintenance bay garage, looking for somebody to give him direction on where to start his second shift.

The maintenance bay was a cavernous garage specifically designed to accommodate the mine's large ore-hauling trucks. It was thirty-five feet high and forty feet wide. Two bays were set side by side and served for general maintenance of the trucks as well as cleaning and repairs. High-powered lights illuminated all aspects of the bay, giving the area a conspicuous and eerie glow to anyone who walked or drove by at night.

Rick could see a truck was already parked in one of the bays. He walked around its front and made his way over to a bench, where he could see another worker sorting through some tools.

"You know where the shift foreman is?" he asked.

The man simply pointed over to two men talking and laughing at a door at the corner of the second bay. Seeing a stripe on both of their hard hats, Rick knew they were foremen. He also knew, as he approached, that one of them was Daryl Rykin.

"Hey, look who we have here," Rykin said. "One part of our two-part clean-up crew. You on my crew now, Torrison, or just double shifting?"

"Double shift," Rick replied. "Blake Thomas said you needed help."

The other foreman waved goodbye to Rykin and let him continue his conversation with Rick. "Damn right we need help," Rykin said. "Every truck that comes in here has to be spick and span for the morning paint! You'll each be using a steam cleaner. It's a sloppy, hot job, Torrison, but someone's gotta do it, right!" Rykin slapped Rick on the back with his usual perverse smile at the pending misery of a worker. "Now, let's go get you into some yellow rain gear and a face shield. We want you looking as pretty going in as going out, Torrison!"

Rykin walked Rick over to a coat rack hung with insulated yellow rain jackets and suspender rain pants. On the shelf above was a set of hard hats equipped with clear face shields, and below each coat was a set of steel-toed rain boots.

As Rick fitted himself, he could already tell why Rykin was smiling about this job. The raincoat felt as heavy as body armour, and he could already feel himself sweating under the rubber coating of the pants. The face shield added awkward weight to his hard hat, and the boots he had on were oversized, causing his feet to slip and rub. *How could it get any worse?* he thought. It did when he came around the back of the truck and saw his partner come out of the cloud of steam and raise his shield.

"Well, fuck me… It's Ricky, right?" Oakey asked as he gave Rick a push on his shoulder with a closed fist.

"Hey, Oakey!" Rick said, trying to be enthusiastic so as to not give Rykin any more pleasure.

"Oakey, get Torrison set up on the other steam cleaner and see if we can get at least two trucks done for the morning. You guys can take your lunch in the cafeteria in a few hours, but if you fall behind, cut it short!" Rykin said with a trumped-up tone of authority. He then turned and walked away with his usual smile on his face.

Oakey was shorter than most workers at the mine, at five foot seven. He was also rounder than most, with a belly that was always held up by a wide belt. He was thirty years old, with a full head of curly brown hair and a flat, broad, and freckled face. His voice was unusually high and only lowered in tone when he was upset or about to lose his temper. In fact, despite his size, many workers refused to work with him because of his temper. It was the main reason the mine and union had agreed to place him alone at the tailings ponds to watch over the pumps.

Oakey rolled over another gas-powered steam cleaner for Rick to use and positioned it near the front of the truck.

"These things pump out scalding-hot water, Rick, so be careful," Oakey said in his high voice. "And forget the dirt. It'll peel the paint right off the fucking truck," he added with an even higher-pitched laugh.

"Thanks, Oakey," Rick said as he squatted to look over the machine for start-up. He looked up. "Hey, Oakey, why are you here cleaning anyway? Who's out at the tailing ponds?"

"Don't know," Oakey said. He then squatted down beside Rick in a manner that suggested they were being watched.

"You know that Rykin is a fucking asshole," he said in a low tone that actually had Rick wondering whether he was talking to the same person.

Rick momentarily blinked his eyes. "Yeah, well, we call him Daryl the Dickhead, Oakey. But why don't we get this cleaning shit done and not give him an excuse to live up to his name."

"Deal!" Oakey said, standing up and returning to his high voice.

Oakey walked around the back of the big truck, where Rick could hear him start up his own cleaner and start working.

Rick turned back to his own machine and started the motor. He pulled his face shield down, grabbed the steam cleaner wand, and started spraying away dirt, and most of the paint with it.

Rick and Oakey worked cleaning the truck for nearly two hours before taking a break. They made good progress, and the good news for both was Rykin was nowhere in sight.

Rick walked over to a side bench located along the maintenance bay wall and sat down for his break. He took off his raincoat, rubber gloves, and hard hat and placed them on the bench beside him. He wiped his forehead with the sleeve of his shirt, and with the arching of his back, he could feel the sweat roll down.

Oakey came over and began to take off his gear. "Why are you wearing that work shirt under the raincoat, Rick?" he asked. Oakey just had his t-shirt on. "Take it off and just wear your undershirt. You won't sweat so much!"

Rick agreed with Oakey's observation and took off his work shirt and kept on his white muscle shirt underneath.

Oakey sat down and reached below the bench. "I've got a big water thermos if you want a drink, Rick."

"Yeah, thanks, Oakey."

Oakey lifted up a large thermos of water and passed it over to Rick. Rick lifted it up and took a big drink from the button spout at the bottom and handed it back to Oakey, who took his own drink.

"Ahhh…I needed that," Rick said. He decided some small talk with Oakey couldn't hurt. "There much to do out at the tailing ponds, Oakey?"

"Not much. Sometimes you get a pump plug or small line break, but most of the time, I just sit in the booth alone, reading a book. Danny Henry, the union rep, got me the job out there. You ever met Danny?"

"Can't say I have," Rick said. "Voted for him like everyone else, but never met the guy in person."

"Well, it can get boring, but Danny said it will keep me out of trouble, and I get paid the same, so I'm not complaining."

"So, why are you here sweating your nuts off to clean a truck?"

Oakey leaned back against the wall, stretched out his legs, and crossed his feet. "Buying me a boat, Rick. And what's your problem? Why are you here?"

Rick copied Oakey's posture.

"Trip to Mexico for my mom at Christmas," Rick replied. "She has MS. It's this disease—"

"Yeah, I know what it is," Oakey said. "My uncle had it. It's a bitch!" He sat up and leaned forward with his arms now resting on his thighs and looked back at Rick. "He lay in bed for two years. Pain, bedsores, cramps, and then one day, he gets pneumonia… Next day, he dies. Fucking MS!"

"Sorry to hear that, Oakey." Rick sat up, looked down at the floor, and dabbed a puddle of water with his boot. He looked back at Oakey. "You said he had cramps? Like, leg cramps? Because my mother gets those all the time. Was there anything you could do for him for that?"

Oakey got up from the bench, let loose a big yawn, and stretched. "Bottles…lots of bottles. Oh shit, here comes Rykin!" he blurted out.

The two men quickly got their gear back on and headed over to the truck. Rykin could be seen approaching the coat rack with the hanging raingear. He had two other workers with him.

Rick and Oakey resumed their cleaning while they watched the two men with Rykin don their own rain suits. Their attention was soon drawn to the bright lights and rumble of a yuke engine announcing the arrival of another truck. The driver stopped briefly at the entrance, gave a few horn blasts, and drove the truck into the bay directly beside Oakey and Rick.

The other two men could be seen rolling out two additional steam cleaning machines, and once they were set up, Rykin left.

Oakey gave the other men a fake wave over the noise of the machines and made his way to Rick at the front of the truck.

Rick saw Oakey coming and put down his wand. He lifted up his face shield. "What's up, Oakey?"

"What the fuck is Rykin doing anyway?" Oakey asked, looking over at the other two men. "He doesn't think we can do two trucks tonight?"

Rick again noticed the distinct octave drop in Oakey's voice. "Ah, he is just worried about his own ass, Oakey. Don't worry about it. They'll have to pay us for the full shift even if we finish early anyway."

"Yeah, but that means less work for us for the rest of the trucks. I need more than a few shifts for my boat." Oakey walked away and left Rick standing without a chance to reply. They didn't talk again until their lunch break at 4 a.m. in the cafeteria.

Milt entered the cafeteria and spotted Rick sitting down at one of the long table benches, eating a hamburger and fries. He walked over, took off his hard hat, and sat down opposite him, straddling the table bench. "Hey, double-shifter…care to share?" he said with a grin.

"What are you doing here?" Rick asked with surprise.

Milt leaned over and stole some of Rick's fries. "I heard through the grapevine you took the double shift, and I also heard you're working for Mr. Dickhead. Came to console you…and eat your fries."

"Yup, you heard right," Rick said, pulling his plate of fries closer. "I'm over in the maintenance bay, cleaning a truck for painting in the morning. Shouldn't you be down in the pit?"

"Just up here to pick up a clamp for a yuke that broke down. Yuke 245…goes down if someone sneezes at it." Milt looked around the cafeteria and spotted Oakey in the food line.

"What's Oakey doing here?" he asked. "Thought he was permanently stuck out at the tailings pond."

"Better than that. He's my partner for cleaning the trucks," Rick said with a chuckle.

Milt quickly turned his head back to Rick. "Fuck off…that maniac?" he said with surprise and concern. "You better not piss him off, Torrison. Something wrong with that guy."

Rick opened a ketchup package and squeezed it out beside his fries. "You know, he's not that bad of a guy. His uncle died of MS. He was having some of the same problems my mom is having now." Rick pushed his plate of fries back toward Milt. "Actually, wouldn't mind talking to him more about it."

"I don't know, Rick. Trouble seems to follow Oakey. I'd be careful."

"Speaking of trouble, I saw Trent Campbell on my way over here to start this shift."

"You can't seem to stay away from that guy, can you? What was it this time? Another grease fight?"

"Actually, no. Just saw him duck into a washroom on the way over here with that stupid duffle bag he is always carrying."

"Yeah…so?" Milt replied as he grabbed Rick's hamburger for a bite. "Told you the guy stinks. Probably trying to wash his clothes in the mine washroom to save money."

"I don't know. He came in just after I left, and there was this guy Santtini in there from the mine parts department. He was carrying something heavy in one of those heavy-duty mine garbage bags. When I went back to get my watch I left on the sink, they were both gone."

Milt placed Rick's half-eaten hamburger down. He changed his straddled sitting position on the bench seat and faced Rick fully. "Rick, who knows what Campbell's up to. The guy lives in what I hear is some run-down cabin on the outside of Tear Falls. He has a wife and son that nobody seems to ever see. Why don't you look on the positive side? He wasn't there when you came back, and you avoided your usual shouting match with him." Milt looked up to see Oakey walking their way. "Besides, I would think one troublemaker is enough."

Oakey had now made his way back over to Milt and Rick and could be seen balancing a food tray in each hand. One tray was stacked high with grilled cheese sandwiches, while the other had a pile of fries with two cans of Coke.

He sat down beside Rick and looked at Milt. "I can't remember your name... Martin?"

Milt spun his hard hat around on the table so his name faced Oakey. "Nope...Milt Tonkin." He waited for his name to register with Oakey from their run-in three years ago when Oakey threatened him with a shovel.

Milt didn't know whether it was forgetfulness or intentional, but Oakey seemed to ignore the connection and put his hand out across the table to shake. "Nice meetin' ya... I'm Oakey," he said, his high voice bringing back memories for Milt. Milt avoided any reference to their previous confrontation and shook Oakey's hand.

Rick turned the conversation back to his mom's MS. "Oakey, you mentioned you used lots of bottles to help with your uncle's cramps from his MS. Like what...vodka...whiskey?"

Oakey laughed. "No! Not fucking booze, Torrison. Hot water bottles! Lots of them. Kept his legs warm at night. My aunt said it helped a lot." Oakey continued to laugh.

Rick and Milt couldn't help but laugh with him.

The three men talked for another half-hour. Oakey even pushed his own plate of fries toward the middle of the table so everyone could share.

He was the first to get up. "Well, I'm going to get one last Coke to go. You guys want one?" he asked. Rick and Milt declined, and Oakey wandered back to the food counter.

Milt stood up and put his hard hat on. "I don't know if that guy has amnesia or what, but he actually doesn't seem all that bad…minus the voice." Milt looked over at Oakey as he made his way through the food line again.

"Yeah, maybe he is meditating or something out there at the tailings pond," Rick said, and he also stood up and put his hard hat on. "You know when he gets all serious or mad, his voice goes really low. It's like two different people. You remember that when he came at you with the shovel?"

"Can't really say I was listening to his voice. Too busy trying to dodge the shovel," Milt said. "Well, I gotta go. Say hi to your mom, and I'll call you about hunting soon."

"See you later."

Oakey soon returned with a Coke in each hand. "If you don't drink it, I will," he said as he handed a Coke to Rick.

The two men began their walk back to the maintenance bay and talked some more. They even joked that bottles of booze might indeed work for MS cramps.

As Rick resumed his steam cleaning, he started to think that the stories of Oakey and his temper might have been overblown. Maybe some of it was just a result of him being teased for his high voice or maybe being overweight. He even thought Milt might have exaggerated the shovel incident. He would only think this for the next two hours.

Rick looked at his watch. It was now 6 a.m., two hours after lunch, and it was time for him and Oakey to take their final coffee break before the end of the shift. He shut down his machine and placed the steam wand in a bracket. He walked around the back of the truck and back up the other side, admiring the two men's cleaning work. *Yup*, he thought, *this truck will definitely be spick and span and ready for paint.* There would be little time to start another truck tonight. Despite Oakey's early objection, he was glad Rykin had recruited the other two men to help out.

Rick caught Oakey's attention and signalled to his watch it was time for break. Oakey gave him a thumbs up through the steam but waved for Rick to start without him.

Rick knew this was Oakey's way of saying he was not stopping work until the other two workers beside them took their break first. He was just too stubborn to let that happen.

Rick walked around the second truck to the bench where he and Oakey had taken their first break. He took off his rain jacket and noticed he was still sweating even with just a white muscle shirt underneath.

He sat down and watched as one of the other workers used a flashlight to check for dirt underneath his truck near his bench.

Suddenly he heard yelling from the other side of the truck. Rick and the worker using the flashlight quickly made their way around to the far side to investigate.

There they could see Oakey and the other worker, shield to shield, yelling at one another. Oakey was pointing to a trail of dirt leading towards their truck while, at the same time, hollering obscenities. Rick ran over and pushed Oakey back while the other man did the same to his partner.

"You're trying to wash all your shit over here!" Oakey yelled out in a deep voice. "It's splashing back up on our truck!"

"Fuck off!" the other worker said. "It's not even close to your truck!"

Rick pushed Oakey back a little further as Oakey continued to yell over his shoulder, "You fuckhead! I'm going to cut your dick off!" He pointed and shook his wand at the other man.

Rick continued to restrain Oakey. "Forget about that asshole, Oakey. We're nearly done."

Oakey lifted up his shield. "I saw that fuck spraying their dirt over here, Rick. He's doing it on purpose. Trying to make us look bad in front of Rykin so they'll get more shifts!"

"C'mon, let's go on break," Rick said, trying to calm Oakey down. "There's nothing Rykin would like more than to catch us fighting."

Oakey seemed to take heed of Rick's words and turned to go shut his own machine down. Rick was about to head back to break when the worker Oakey had been arguing with purposely sprayed some dirt up from the floor. The dirt splattered across the back of Oakey's yellow rain pants as he walked in the opposite direction.

Oakey turned around in a rage and immediately ran past Rick. He swung his steam cleaning wand and sprayed scalding hot water at the other man. Rick ran to grab Oakey, but in the chaos, he stepped on Oakey's high-pressure hose. There was a snap, and the hose broke off, recoiling back like a snake and spewing scalding water across Rick's chest and left arm. His muscle shirt offered little protection, and he yelled out in pain as the hot water immediately inflicted first- and second-degree burns. He screamed, "Ah fuck, Oakey!"

Oakey stopped and ran back to Rick, who was on his knees and bent over in agony. He could already see blistering red skin on Rick's left arm. "Holy shit, Rick!" he yelled as he tried to lift him up. "Somebody get my jug of cold water!"

One worker ran for the water while the other ran to turn off Oakey's machine and call emergency.

Rick was taken to the mine emergency medical room, where he was treated, and by the end of the shift, he was resting in the back of an ambulance from Tear Falls Hospital. The sun had now risen, and he could see through the ambulance windows the workers coming off shift and boarding the buses home. Even though they were a few blocks away, Rick could see many of them turning their heads to look at the flashing ambulance lights. He was sure he recognized the long hair of Milt as being one of them.

Four days after the accident, Rick lay in his hospital bed and waited for the doctor and a nurse to make their usual rounds to give him an update. Three-quarters of his left arm was wrapped in bandages, and one large bandage covered the top portion of his chest. He had reddened areas on his face and right arm but nothing serious enough to warrant a dressing. The pain was now controlled, and he was beginning to eat normally again. His next-door neighbour had already brought his mother by for a visit and told Rick she would take care of any extra help his mother needed until he came home.

Rick heard a knock at the door. He expected the doctor, but instead, in walked a smiling Roddy Simone and Milt.

"Hey, there's the hero!" Roddy said as he reached out and gently shook Rick's right hand.

Milt came around the same side of the bed and gave Rick a smile.

"Hero…? I don't think so," Rick replied. "More like a stupid move at a stupid time!"

"You sure?" Roddy asked as he and Milt grabbed two chairs and turned them backwards to sit down. Roddy reached into his back pocket, took out a piece of paper, and eyed some numbers on it as he said, "I heard you were saving Jasmine Rubuwen from a pot of hot coffee in the cafeteria. At least, that's what your buddy Milt here says."

Rick looked at Milt, who winked. "Yeah…let's go with that one. What's the story going around the mine on what happened, Milt?" he asked with concern.

"Usual rumour shit," Milt said. "Some people think it was a fight between you and Oakey. Others have Oakey fighting all three of you, and some people even have you guys all fighting Rykin. Sorry to say, nothing about you saving Jasmine comes up."

"Any of the others back at work?" Rick asked.

"Haven't seen any of them. Imagine they have all been suspended. Wouldn't be surprised if Oakey gets fired. They've been waiting for some time to get rid of him. Union rep. hasn't been around to see you yet?"

"Not yet. But I'm sure he'll be around with news and the paperwork soon." Rick grabbed a capped foam cup with a straw and took a long drink of water. "Never know, Milt. Union rep could come in tomorrow and say I'm fired, too." Rick lay back on his pillow. "Any way you look at it, I ain't going back to the mine. I have no money coming in, and I can kiss my mom's Christmas trip to Mexico and any treatment at that Tijuana MS clinic goodbye."

Milt and Roddy looked at each other, silent. Roddy folded up the paper he had in his hand and placed it back in his pocket. They knew what Rick was saying was most likely the truth.

Chapter Six

# THINK POSITIVE

Rick came home after five days in the hospital, and although the doctor had said he might have some scarring on his left arm, everyone agreed the healing process was going much better than expected. The bandages covering his left arm and chest were much smaller now, but he still only wore muscle shirts for the comfort they provided on movement.

Rick paced back and forth in his mother's living room, waiting for Danny Henry, the mine's union rep to arrive at the door. Danny said he would be at Rick's home around 10 a.m., but by 10:05, Rick was already nervously checking the window and worrying Danny wouldn't show.

The sound of a car running over the gravel of the driveway signalled Danny had arrived. Rick was quick to open the front door even as Danny was still reaching for his black briefcase out of the back seat of his car.

"Morning, Rick!" Danny yelled as he walked to the front door. "Got the coffee ready?"

Danny Henry was fifty years old and near Rick's height and weight. He was from the native reserve of Crescent Lake but had lived just outside of Tear Falls for the past twenty-six years. He had long black hair streaked with some grey that was kept in a neat ponytail. He had a slightly darker complexion reflective of his Ojibwa heritage and was known for his large blue eyes, which always caught everyone's attention.

Rick let Danny in the door, and they shook hands. Rick directed him towards the kitchen. "Coffee, you said?" he asked nervously.

"Be great if you have it, Rick," Danny replied. He sat down and opened up his briefcase. He set out two piles of papers so both he and Rick could go through things together.

"Your mother not up yet, Rick?" he asked as he looked around.

"No, she is sleeping," Rick said. "She was up at seven but back to bed by nine. She rests a lot during the day."

Rick brought over two black coffees and pointed to cream and sugar already on the table for Danny. He sat down and began to speak without even looking at the papers Danny had passed over to him. "Well, all I need to know, Danny, is whether I have a job or if I am going on welfare."

Danny stirred his coffee. "Guess it's a yes and no, Rick. The mine has suspended you and the two other guys working on the other truck."

"And Oakey?"

"Gone…fired," Danny said. "He's already gone back to Crescent Lake. But you probably already guessed that. We all knew management was gunning for Oakey." He sipped his coffee.

"I never knew Oakey was…" Rick reached for the right words.

"Ojibwa…native….an injun…?" Danny said, chuckling. "Not all of us have to look the way you think we should, Rick." He handed Rick a piece of paper that described his rights upon termination from Rennet Mine, including possible severance.

Danny could tell Rick felt uncomfortable with what he'd said about Oakey. He leaned forward and rested his forearms on the table. "Look, don't worry about it, Rick. I'm used to being and looking out for the disadvantaged. Why do you think I'm so good at this job? I know your mother has MS, and I know you took on extra work with Rocelli because of it."

Danny sat up and pointed at the termination paper in Rick's hand. "Take a look at that termination information. I'll be honest and tell you it's highly likely they're going to fire you. They were just waiting for you to come out of the hospital for their own PR, but I will do everything to try and keep you on and, if not, make the mine pay. It's the least I can do as your union representative."

"Thanks, Danny. I appreciate what you're doing for me, but it sounds like there is not much hope," Rick replied. His nervousness was now replaced by dejection.

"Maybe… Maybe not," Danny said. "Let me do my job, and we'll see where it goes." He took another piece of paper out of his briefcase, this one labelled "Employee Incident Report," and took out a pen.

"Rick, I would like you to explain to me exactly what happened that night. I'm going to write everything down, and this is what I will take to management next week as a part of my meeting."

Rick recounted the night's events for Danny, starting with the beginning of the shift, talking with Rykin, and going right through to him being taken away in an ambulance. Danny asked a few questions and asked for a few pauses so he could catch up on writing, but within a half-hour, they were done.

"Good," Danny said. "I think that's enough for today. You have any other questions right now, Rick?"

Rick looked down at the stack of paperwork in front of him and flipped through the corners with his thumb. "Let me ask you something, Danny."

"Shoot."

"What's a guy get for stealing from the mine?"

"Stealing…? I guess that would depend on what it was and how much. Why do you ask?"

Rick looked back up at Danny. "I don't know. I guess I see a guy like me who gets into an accident trying to stop another one from probably happening, winds up in the hospital with burns, makes a good recovery, and basically has been a hardworking employee all his life, and all they want to do is get rid of me." Rick tapped his stack of paper with his middle finger. "Just wondering if I would have been better off stealing and at least made some money for my mom's care."

Danny could see the frustration on Rick's face. The anger in his voice was palpable. "If you are asking me if the system is unfair, Rick, I will be the first person to tell you it's more than unfair. It's purposely stacked against you. Rennet doesn't give a rat's ass about what you did or how hard you work. They saw a chance to get rid of Oakey, and they took it. You're just the white man thrown out with the big bad Indian bathwater."

Danny leaned back in his chair and put a hand on his own stack of paper. "But you see, Rick, this is all I got to fight back against that shit. For good people like you, Oakey, and every other employee at Rennet, all I can do is make sure that they follow the rules."

Rick shook his head. "And it's their fucking rules. No different than the care of my mom, Danny."

"Probably not," Danny replied. He sat up in his chair, placed his hands on his thighs, and looked straight at Rick. "But you know what, Rick? I'm pretty good at making them pay for it!"

Rick cracked a smile. "Well, I'm glad you're on my side, Danny. Whatever happens."

Danny stood up. "It's in my job description, Rick, but probably more importantly, in my nature," he said with a smile. "Anything more before I go?"

"No. I'll call you if there is anything else."

Danny pointed at the paperwork in front of Rick. "There are the reports from the other men in there if you care to read them. The two men working opposite you didn't have anything nice to say, but Oakey did his best to make you look good. Can't fault the man for going down swinging."

"Well, if you see him, thank him for me, Danny. Oakey is a good guy."

"I'll make sure to do that, Rick."

Rick escorted Danny to the door and thanked him again. Then he went back to the kitchen and opened the fridge to take out a beer. He sat down at the table and casually flipped through the paperwork, trying to think of what he was going to do. What would he do without the mine income? What would he do without benefits? And what would he do in order to take care of his mother? He smiled to himself at the thought of how Milt could "go better" and spin this situation into a positive. There was no way. Rick immediately got up and phoned Paul Rocelli.

## Chapter Seven

# NAKED BEAR

Rick sat in the Lake Fuels truck on the airport tarmac, alternating between looking down at his watch and looking up at the night sky. It was now 8:20 p.m., twenty minutes past the scheduled arrival time for the Twin Otter passenger plane, and his agitation was beginning to build. He had to get home to relieve the hired help for his mom by 10 p.m., or the extra hours Paul had given him would go to paying her overtime. The airport was now pitch-black with the exception of the runway lights and a few lights glowing off the main terminal building. It was more than dark enough for him to spot the lights of a plane heading in for a landing, but he saw nothing.

"Where the fuck is that fuckin' plane?" he said.

As Danny Henry had predicted, the Rennet Mine had terminated Rick's employment shortly after their meeting at his home. Danny had argued as best he could, but it was an easy decision for mine management. Rick had only been at Rennet Mine for three years, so his severance was minimal. More importantly, he was necessary collateral damage so there would be no controversy about the firing of Oakey. Danny did manage to squeeze out a few concessions and get Rick six months of extended rent in their mine-owned house, but essentially, he left with three weeks' pay and nothing more.

Rick looked at his watch again: 8:30 p.m. He couldn't wait any longer. He was getting out of the truck to walk to the main terminal to get an arrival update when he saw the lights of two vehicles come through the airport gates and onto the tarmac. He paused at the bottom of the truck's stairs and stared. He was wondering who had access this late at night to a restricted airport area. The two vehicles stopped approximately five hundred feet away and were unrecognizable in the glare of their headlights.

Rick walked slowly toward the terminal, all the while keeping his focus on the two sets of headlights. With a sudden flicker, the vehicle lights dimmed and turned off. He could now see the first vehicle was a heavy-duty van of a dark colour. But it was the second vehicle that surprised him. Even in the moonlight, he could see the letters glowing off the side of the second vehicle: O.P.P. It was the Ontario Provincial Police.

"Hey, Rick! What's the matter with you?" a young Randy Biggs yelled out in the dark.

"What...?" Rick was caught off guard by Randy's voice.

Randy Biggs approached close enough for Rick to see him. "I said what's the matter with you? You look like you've seen a bear... naked!" Randy said with a laugh.

Randy Biggs was the airport's jack-of-all-trades employee. He was only twenty-two years old, and he fixed things, loaded baggage, and swept floors. Most often, though, he was the airport's makeshift version of security. Randy enjoyed the night shift because few people were around. He enjoyed it even more because he was often stoned.

"No, I'm good, Randy," Rick replied. "Hey, what's going on over there with the van and the police?"

Randy took a look, shading his eyes with his hand for no reason. "Looks like the cops. Don't go over there, or they are going to shoot you!" Randy laughed again.

Rick could tell Randy was high and had little interest in the two parked vehicles, even if one of them was the police.

"Rick, I just came out to tell you there is no plane tonight. Mechanical problems or something, so it won't be arriving until tomorrow morning. So, hows about yous and I go get some chips out of the snack machine for a break?"

"Ah, I don't think so, Randy. I need to get home to my mom. Thanks anyway." Rick split off from Randy with a wave and headed toward the Lake Fuels office. He stepped in, immediately walked over to a window, and continued to watch the two vehicles parked silently at the other end of the tarmac. After ten minutes of no activity, he decided he had to go or he would be late to relieve his mom's help. He placed his work clothes in the office locker, grabbed his brown leather jacket, and changed his footwear to his familiar white Adidas runners with the red stripes. He posted a note for Paul on the bulletin board that the last flight of the night had been cancelled, and then he headed out to the airport parking lot.

He drove his car slowly out of the parking lot even though it was well lit and almost empty. He was still trying to catch a glimpse of any activity around the vehicles he was watching, but the best he could do was see Randy sitting in the near dark on the terminal steps, eating a bag of chips.

He drove on and eventually stopped at the highway turnoff two miles down the road. He'd started to look both ways for a left turn when his eyes caught the navigation lights of a plane coming in to land at the airport. He waited for a moment and could determine it was likely a twin-engine Cessna, but he wondered why the flight had not been noted in the airport flight schedule. He looked out again, waiting for the plane to come closer to see if it had lighted markings he could identify. As the plane flew over, his concentration was broken by the horn of a pickup truck behind him. "Take it easy, buddy," he said. He waved back at the driver and turned to head home.

Chapter Eight

# COFFEE WITH ABIGAIL

It was now mid-October, and Rick and Milt had agreed to meet at the Abby Corner Cafe for a 9 a.m. Saturday breakfast. It was one of the few dates their days off coincided, and Milt was anxious to catch up on news and see if they could schedule some hunting.

Rick walked into the cafe to find Milt already sitting on one of the green counter stools, drinking a coffee. With the weather getting colder, Milt was now wearing a Boston Bruins hockey toque in place of his usual hat and a heavy grey sweater underneath his jean jacket.

Rick and Milt had been coming to the Abby Corner Cafe since they were big enough to push money across the counter to buy fries. The restaurant had been built in the forties, and it still retained much of the original decor. A large, conspicuous Coca-Cola sign hung on a pole outside, with the Abby Corner Cafe name clearly visible underneath. Abigail was the name of the owner's only daughter, and it had been his hope that she would eventually take over the business. Years later, he would joke that she went and did something stupid like go to university to be a lawyer. She never returned to Tear Falls, and even though the cafe was sold in the late sixties, the new owners had kept the name for its familiarity around town.

"Couldn't have ordered me a coffee, could you? Ya cheap bastard," Rick said with a smile as he sat down on the stool next to Milt.

"You worth a coffee?" Milt said. He signalled the waitress for another. "How's Rocelli treating you?"

"Taking all the hours I can, but even with that, it's not going to keep up with the bills. Doctor is now recommending my mom get a hospital bed if she is to stay at home. You ever seen the cost of one of those?"

Rick paused his conversation as the waitress came over with his coffee and the two men ordered their breakfasts.

"They also had a therapist see her at the doctor's office to help with her feeding herself. You know she is having a hard time even holding onto a fork now?" Rick said as he picked up his own from his place setting. "Can you imagine that, Milt? A stupid fork! She can't even hold onto to this stupid fucking fork!"

Milt had seen little of Rick since his firing from the mine from a few months ago. They would try to meet up, but either the two men would be on a different shift schedule or Rick would be called into work by Rocelli at the last minute and would cancel. They settled for talks on the phone, but even in these conversations, Milt could feel the stress and anxiety building in Rick's voice over his mom's deteriorating health. Now, in the cafe, he could see it in person. Rick had let his short brown hair become long and unkempt. He noticed he had on dirty work boots instead of his favourite white Adidas runners with the red stripes. Even Rick's prized brown leather jacket was now stained with gas.

"Wow..." Milt said. "I didn't know things were getting that bad."

Rick placed his elbows on the counter and took a minute to rub the tiredness from his face.

He turned to face Milt. "Yup...it's that bad, Milt. And you know what? The worrying never stops. I used to worry about her cramps in the night. Now I'm worried about her being able to drink a glass of water or eat her dinner and two-thousand-dollar fucking hospital beds."

Milt rubbed his coffee handle with his thumb. "You know the offer from Kristen and I still stands. A few thousand could help pay for a hospital bed. I know Roddy was trying to help. Maybe Kristen and I can work something out with him through the NearNorth?"

"Ah shit, it's more than that, Milt! I know Roddy was trying to help, but my mom's going downhill no matter how many two-thousand-dollar hospital beds I buy! What I need is two hundred thousand dollars for that clinic in Mexico Eduardo told me about. Where am I going to get that money, Milt? Money to cure her! Not die in a fucking hospital bed!" Rick slammed his fist down on the counter hard enough to cause other customers to look over.

The waitress reappeared with their orders of bacon and eggs and placed them in front of the two men.

"Everything alright here?" she asked with concern.

"Fine," Milt said. "He's just a bit hungry."

Rick shook his head as the waitress left. "Sorry about that, Milt. I just don't know what I'm going to do." He rubbed the palms of his hands together. "Hey, let's talk about something different! Tell me what's going on at the mine these days."

Milt was happy to change the conversation and bring Rick up to speed on the latest Rennet Mine news. He told him Rykin was still a dickhead and explained how he had still managed to dodge any crew shift changes. He told Rick about Trent Campbell being transferred to Oakey's old position out at the tailings pond, which, he was relieved to see, actually brought a smile to Rick's face.

It was not long before the conversation switched to Rick's job, and Rick started relaying to Milt the story about the two vehicles and the unknown plane.

"I'm telling you, Milt, I think it must have been a load of gold from the Stinson Mine they were shipping out that night. Why else would there be a police car? Why else the unrecorded flight?" he asked.

"Might have been," Milt said. "Like I said at the bar, not like they're going to advertise it."

"Yeah, but it doesn't seem like all that much security for a gold shipment. One cop car and a cargo van?"

"That's it?" Milt asked. "What about airport security?"

"Ah, they got this guy, Randy Biggs, but he is stoned all the time. Hard to believe he could secure anything."

"Well, I think you got it all wrong. First off, who around here is going to steal gold bars? What would you do with them? Not like you could go buy something."

"Well, what about some out-of-town thieves wanting to rip it off?" Rick asked.

"And go where?" Milt argued. "It takes more than two hours down Highway 205 to even get close to another major highway. The cops would have that blocked off in no time. Not worth it!"

"Yeah...you might be right. Still, would be interesting if that was the Stinson gold plane."

"Well, the next time you see it, go over and ask the cop and see what he says," Milt said, finishing his coffee. He looked at his watch. "Well, I got to go. Kid's hockey practice in an hour."

"Hey, no problem," Rick said. He grabbed Milt's arm as he went to get up. "Thanks for listening, Milt. I know I haven't been much of a friend lately. Let's go hunting soon."

"Promise?" Milt asked.

"Guaranteed!" Rick replied.

Milt got into his parked pickup truck, and even though he had to get to his son's hockey practice, he needed a minute to absorb Rick's change in appearance and outburst in the cafe. He was now officially worried.

## Chapter Nine

# EXPENSES

A week after the breakfast with Milt, Rick was sitting in the Lake Fuels office on a Saturday, his feet up on the desk, eating wieners and beans out of a thermos for lunch. He heard a loud rapping at the door and looked up to see a waving Randy Biggs asking him to open up.

Rick got up with a confused look and let Randy in. "What's the matter?" he asked.

Breathing heavily, Randy rushed over to the window facing the runway and motioned for Rick to follow. "Have I got something to show you!" he said with an excited smile on his face.

Rick came over and looked out across the tarmac. There, in the distance, he saw the same dark-coloured van he had observed a week ago. But now he could see four men in work jackets loading crates into the cargo hold of a twin-engine Cessna.

Rick looked at Randy. "Stinson Mine gold?"

"Fucking right!" Randy said. "And by the looks of things, I'd say at least ten crates have gone into that plane so far." Randy walked over to a drawer on the far side of the office and took out a pair of binoculars. He walked back and gave them to Rick.

"Hey, how did you know—" Rick tried to ask.

"Never mind… Take a closer look."

Rick looked through the binoculars and watched the men loading the crates.

"But where are the cops, and why in the morning? I thought they did this stuff under the cover of darkness?" Rick handed the binoculars back to Randy to take a look.

"Cops were here. They left," Randy said. "I guess they get bored and fucked off as soon as they started loading." Randy put the binoculars down. "I talked to another pilot who said the flights come in once a week, but the times are always different. The pilot said they do that on purpose so no one can plan ahead to rob the gold from the van or the plane."

"Well, that makes sense," Rick replied. "Can't have a bunch of guys with guns hanging out in the terminal all day just waiting."

Rick took the binoculars from Randy for another look. *Finally, the vehicles and the unknown plane from the other night make sense,* he thought.

For the rest of the day, with the exception of the little excitement with Randy and the Stinson Mine gold, everything was routine. At the end of the shift, he'd just sat down to record the day's fuel billings when the office phone rang.

"Lake Fuels!" he answered.

To Rick's surprise, it was Milt on the other end of the line. He explained to Rick his mom had fallen and the hired house help had been unable to reach him so she had called him as an emergency contact. His mom had been taken to the Tear Falls Hospital, and he should head over there as soon as possible.

Rick hung up the phone and quickly took off his coveralls. He threw them into the office locker, grabbed his leather jacket, and headed to the hospital.

He arrived at 6 p.m., and the short fall day had already made the parking lot dark. He rushed to the nurse's station and asked to see his mother. A nurse led him to his mother's room and told him she was sedated and resting comfortably. The left side of her face was swollen, and her left arm was bruised, but the nurse assured him nothing was broken. She told Rick there would be a meeting in the morning regarding his mother's condition and they were hoping he would attend. Rick thanked her, and she left the room. He sat down in a chair, held his mother's hand, and said a prayer.

Rick returned to the hospital shortly after 9 a.m. the next morning and went straight to his mother's room. He found her alert and sitting up in bed, eating breakfast. She now had braces on both her wrists to help her hold her knife and fork. He came in and gave her a big hug, and he told her that everything was going to be okay and he was going to a meeting at 9:30 a.m. to discuss getting her home. His mother said she was doing fine and was never worried with him taking care of her.

At 9:30 a.m., Rick made his way to a small hospital conference room down the hall. He walked into the room and saw an oval table with a laminate wood grain top. Ten bright blue cushion chairs encircled the table. A nurse and a doctor were arranging some paperwork on the table, and a third woman, whom Rick didn't recognize, was standing beside them.

The nurse came over to Rick and introduced herself.

"Hi, I am Chantel Bryson, one of the nurses looking after your mother, and I believe you're…Rick?"

"That's right," Rick said, although he was sure they knew each other from his stay at the hospital for his burns. He recognized the man as Dr. Siller, who worked at the hospital but who was also his mother's family doctor.

"Please, have a seat," Chantel said.

Rick went to take off his leather jacket, but then he became acutely aware he was underdressed and far from presentable. Underneath his leather jacket, he was wearing a blue work-stained sweatshirt from the day before, and beneath that was the ripped collar of a white t-shirt. He even took a moment to feel his hair, which hadn't been washed in three days, and it was now so long that its waves would often drop in front of his face. He wondered whether the hospital would think he was having a hard enough time taking care of himself, let alone his mother. He pushed his hair back with his hand as best he could and sat down with his leather jacket on.

Dr. Siller sat down with the others and began the meeting.

"Thanks for coming in, Rick. I believe you know me and you have met Nurse Bryson. I would also like to introduce you to Margaret Seaver, who is our newly hired social worker here at the hospital."

Rick smiled at everyone, and Dr. Siller continued.

"Rick, we wanted to first tell you your mom's fall might look bad, but it's mostly bruising that will quickly heal. And we're pretty sure she can go home in a few days."

"Well, that's good news."

"Very good news. But our biggest concern is the general deterioration in her overall condition, Rick. It's accelerating, and we're thinking your mother may have to consider other options for her care."

"Like...?" Rick said, his face becoming tense.

Margaret Seaver jumped in, saying, "Well, Rick, we were thinking of you and your mom discussing placement in the local Tear Falls nursing home. I know it sounds drastic, but all the medical reports say falls like this are going to happen more often, and maybe with worse results for your mother."

Rick bridged his fingers on the table. "Well, I'll just hire more help, then. Hire a nurse who is trained in MS."

"It's more than that, Rick," Chantel Bryson said. "Here's a list of recommendations from the hospital for when she goes home." She passed Rick the report. "You can see on there she should have a commode beside her bed, and probably some bars in her bathroom to grab onto, and maybe even a small ramp at your front door for a wheelchair. And that's the small stuff. We think there is also the need for a hospital bed and maybe an expensive specialized electric wheelchair."

Rick took the list. There were a few minutes of silence as he looked it over. He looked up. "She needs all this? Well, maybe I can make some of it." He threw the list to the centre of the table.

Dr. Siller tried his turn. "Rick, there is also the issue of your mom being able to feed herself. She can do it right now, but it's becoming more difficult. And there's always the risk of choking, something staff in nursing homes are trained to deal with. We're also worried about how her care is now taking a toll on you. If you were to get sick, then what would happen with your mother's care?"

Rick got the distinct sense the meeting was not a discussion but a directive. He was starting to feel cornered. He gripped the chair's armrests. "Can I ask you people something? Can I ask where the cure is for all this…like the MS? Because all I see coming from everyone is buy this, buy that, but guess what? It's only going to prolong the inevitable. And by the way, if you want to stop the leg cramps, buy this medicine for two hundred dollars. Two hundred dollars a month!"

"That's why we thought maybe the nursing home would be a better choice," Chantel Bryson said, trying to reassure Rick. "The government would then pay for most of her medications, and they have all the medical equipment she would need."

"Bullshit!" Rick rebutted. "She would get worse in a nursing home!" He stood up and pushed his chair back from the table. "Meeting over! When she's ready, I'll take her home." He made his way to the door.

"Rick…we're just trying to help," Dr. Siller called after him.

Rick turned at the conference room doorway. "Help…for her to rot away in a nursing home? You call that help?" He took a few steps back into the room. "I will tell you what helps! Fifty-cent hot water bottles, that's what fucking helps!"

He slammed the door and headed back to his mother's room. Once there, he decided not to tell his mother the details of his disagreement with Dr. Siller or the others at the morning meeting.

Instead, he said he was working on a plan to have her come home and that he would be back to visit soon.

He returned home, still upset about the morning meeting. He took a beer out of the fridge and had just sat down to write down the list of things that were on the hospital medical report when the phone rang.

"Hello?"

"Hey, Ricardo! How you doing, my friend!" Rick knew immediately from the Spanish accent and distant sound it was Eduardo from the Larga Vida Villa in Mexico.

"Hey, Eduardo. How are things in Mexico!?" Rick was glad to be distracted from the day's events. "Why the call? You haven't been deported to Canada, have you?"

"No...no...Too cold for me, amigo. Hey, I'm calling because you haven't booked your room with your mom yet. I don't want to give it away after all these years. Anything wrong? You still coming for Christmas?"

"Yeah, Eduardo, my mom isn't doing so well. I'm going to see in the next few days whether we can come. Can you hold it that long?"

"Oh yeah...no problem. For you, Rick, I will say it's booked. Call me when you know. Just wanted to make sure you hadn't drowned in some snow!" Eduardo said with a laugh.

"Not yet." Rick replied, laughing back. He was about to thank Eduardo for taking the time to call when he decided to ask him about the clinic in Tijuana.

"Eduardo, I don't want to take up more money on long distance, but you know that clinic you keep saying could help my mom...like, even cure her?"

"Yes...San Judas Hospital. They have helped lots of people like your mom. Expensive, Rick. You need to bring your house with you. Some people say twenty thousand of your dollars just to start!"

"Yeah, well, maybe I will sell it and bring the money," Rick replied, not wanting to admit the mine house was rented.

Eduardo could detect the concern in Rick's voice. "Do you want me to check, Rick? Mothers are worth all the money."

"Would help, Eduardo. Gives me one more reason to make sure she makes the trip this year. I'll start thinking about where to get the extra money here."

"Will do, my friend. Maybe you can call me in a few weeks and tell me about the room, too."

"For sure, Eduardo. You will hear from me." Rick thanked Eduardo and hung up the phone. Then he sat back down at the table and returned to his list from the hospital, trying to estimate costs and things he could do himself.

After a few minutes, his concentration was broken by thoughts of what Eduardo had said about the twenty thousand dollars for the hospital. He stood up and threw his pencil down in frustration. He walked into the living room and opened a wooden tabletop Lazy Susan and took out a bottle of rye. He took the bottle back into the kitchen, poured several ounces into a glass, and started working on some other figures.

At 5 p.m., the doorbell rang at the front door. Rick sat up from lying on the living room couch and took a moment to orient himself from a rye-induced sleep. The doorbell rang again, and he heard the door open. He looked up to see Milt's wife, Kristen, walk by with a large box in her arms.

"Hi, Rick!" Kristen said as she headed straight for the kitchen. Rick pushed himself off the couch and followed.

"Thought you would like a ready-made supper," she said. She placed the box on the kitchen counter and started unpacking various covered dishes. She turned around and gave Rick a once-over. "Are you okay, Rick? Is Rocelli working you that hard?"

"Yeah…why? Do I look that bad?" he replied, feeling his head of tangled hair and looking down at his stained white muscle shirt.

"Well…no. I guess not." Kristen returned to unpacking the box. "Just take care of yourself, alright?"

"I will… Probably just overtired."

Kristen opened up a few drawers and cupboards, took out a place setting for Rick, and brought the items to the table. She picked up some of Rick's afternoon paperwork. "What's this?" she asked with a smile. "Gold prices, crate numbers, troy ounces… what, are you cooking something for a king or going prospecting?"

"Just…well, thinking of investing… I don't know," Rick said. He took the papers out of her hands and threw them in the garbage. "Stupid idea anyway."

"Stupid or not, you gotta eat," Kristen said as she finished setting everything out for Rick. "There. Now, is your mom feeling better?"

"Not bad. Hoping to have her home in a few days."

"Good. If you need any extra help from me or Milt for when she gets home, you let us know."

"I will."

"Well, I better get home and get dinner ready for my own family. You can heat up the food whenever you are ready, and put any leftovers in the fridge so they don't go bad."

"Thanks, Kristen. And tell Milt I haven't forgot about hunting."

"I will tell him."

Kristen gave Rick a hug and a kiss and headed out the door.

Rick walked back to the trash can and fished out his numbers on the Stinson Mine gold shipments. Once he had estimated the number of crates of gold in each plane, the weight of each gold bar in a crate, and the current price of gold, he came to what he thought was probably a fairly accurate figure of the value of each shipment. He circled a number at the bottom of the wrinkled piece of paper: "475,000."

Rick came in the following day to Lake Fuels for his regular 7:30 a.m. shift. When he went to unlock the office door, though, it slid open without him turning the key. He cautiously walked inside and was surprised to see Paul Rocelli already there and sitting at his desk.

"Hey, Rick. C'mon in. Have a seat," Paul said. Rick sat down and, as was the norm, waited for Paul to finish his paperwork. After a few minutes, Paul looked up. "How's your mom?"

"She's still in the hospital. They think maybe a week and I can take her home. Thanks for asking, and thanks for giving me yesterday off," Rick replied.

"Hey, if anyone knows about taking care of sick parents, it's me, right?"

The whistling of a small espresso coffee maker on the office hot plate drew both men's attention. Paul walked over and took the coffee pot off the hot element. "Coffee, Rick? I mean real coffee!" he added with a smile.

"Sure," Rick said, grinning back.

Paul poured the coffee into two small espresso cups and gave one to Rick. He sat back down.

"Rick, I have some bad news. And I know this hurts all the more considering what you are going through with your mom, but we have had some cutbacks on our regular flights."

Rick took a sip of his espresso, wishing it was now rye. "What kind of cutbacks?"

"The regular passenger flights. The company operating them says the demand just isn't there anymore for two or three flights a day. Looks like they are going down to one a day during the week and one on Saturday. No Sunday flights."

"Wow." Rick finished his coffee and placed the cup on Paul's desk. "And that means what for me?" he asked, anticipating the worst.

"Well, they're not going to make the changes until after the busy Christmas travel season, but I'll be honest, Rick. I think we are looking at your last day sometime the third week of December."

Rick leaned back in his chair. "I understand, Paul. It's not your fault. I appreciate you giving me the heads up. Actually, it might work out because my mom and I go to Mexico every year for Christmas. I'll try and make the best of it and look on the bright side."

"Well, I'm really sorry, Rick," Paul said. "Hey, what about looking for a job at the Stinson Gold mine? They always seem to be doing good."

"Yeah, I will check them out," Rick said. He paused for a moment. "Speaking of which, their plane, Paul...how come we never have to fuel it up?"

"Ah, it's all about security, Rick. They have modified tanks, no passenger seats. All cargo. They can fly across the country without refuelling. Personally, I think it's just because they're cheap and don't want to pay our prices." Paul laughed, and Rick nodded in agreement.

Paul got up from his chair, came around the desk, and put a hand on Rick's shoulder. "Rick, you've done a good job here. You learned fast. More than happy to put in a good word for you for whatever comes up!"

"Thanks, Paul," Rick replied, standing up. "Well, I'm going to go out and check the tanks. You sticking around?"

"No, I've got some town fuel runs to do. But I'll be back tomorrow. Can you work the day after tomorrow? I have to take my dad to a doctor's appointment out of town."

"Yeah...no problem. Give me all the hours you want now, Paul!"

Rick stopped by the hospital to visit his mom on the way home, and he could see she was recovering well. He kept the news of his pending layoff from Lake Fuels to himself and instead concentrated on talking about how they were still going away at Christmas to Mexico. They talked about the beach, the nice breeze, and the warm water, but Rick knew it was all for nought if her health continued to deteriorate.

After an hour, he said goodbye to his mom with a smile, but in reality, he was more distressed than ever. He came home and decided to pour himself half a glass of rye and take a hot shower as a means to decompress.

He stood in the shower and watched the excess water fill the empty rye glass sitting on the shower floor. He thought about how to tell his mother that they were not going to Mexico, that he'd lost his job and, that the hospital had recommended she be moved to a nursing home. He thought of Eduardo and the twenty-thousand-dollar Mexican hospital. He imagined Oakey's uncle dying of MS in his sleep. He took a deep breath and leaned his head back into the shower.

"Fuck...that's not going to happen to my mother."

Chapter Ten

# HIGH NEWS

Rick woke up the next morning of his visit to his mother in the hospital with renewed energy. He made himself a coffee and immediately went down to his wooden homemade workbench in the basement. He took out a large map of North America and spread it across the bench top. He pulled out old boxes and took out as many books as he could that would have information on the Cessna airplane, and he stacked them beside the map. He opened one of the bench drawers and took out two pins and some string. Then he placed one pin on Tear Falls and another on Tijuana Mexico. He stretched the string between the two pins and then marked it with a pen according to the scale on the map. He'd started to do some calculations with a pencil on the map border when he noticed his hand was shaking. If he were going to steal the Stinson gold plane and fly it to Mexico, he better make it.

Rick now made a point of chatting up the pilots of any Cessna planes he fueled up. He showed them his bush pilots license, which provided an immediate bond so they were more than willing to answer his questions and show him around the plane. He wrote notes on everything they said and placed them under his work clipboard to take home. One pilot even gave him a spare manual. The only thing Rick had not been able to write notes on was the Stinson gold plane. He had not seen the plane in over a week.

Rick was sitting in the Lake Fuels office for the end of another weekend evening shift, writing up his time sheet. He filled in his hours and the date of November 10 and did a nervous roll tap with the fingers of his other hand on the desk. He was overdue to call Eduardo back, and only after some negotiations had he delayed his mom's discharge from the hospital. He placed the form in a tray and walked over to the window. There was some light snow coming down, but otherwise, it was a quiet night. No van, no police, and no Stinson plane. He was just about to turn to go home when Randy Biggs jumped up on the other side of the window.

"Boo!" Randy yelled.

Rick recoiled with fright. "What the fuck, Randy...! What are you doing?"

"Hold on...coming around," Randy said.

He came to the front office door, and Rick let him in. Then he took off a pair of red mitts, his grey toque, and a heavy blue parka and placed them all on the side of the office desk. "Scared the shit out of ya, didn't I!" he said, laughing.

"Yeah, you did that much," Rick said. "Why are you sneaking around the office? You calling that security again?"

Randy sat down in the office guest chair, his heavy snowmobile boots creating a thud as he stretched his legs out and rested them on the floor.

"Nope. I'm here because I heard the bad news and I'm going to make it better for you, Rick!" he said, laughing again.

Rick sat in the office chair and leaned forward to look closer at Randy's eyes. "Are you fucking stoned again, Randy? You know, one of these days, they're going to catch up to you and toss your ass for that."

"Not a chance, Rick!" Randy said. "I'm too smart for them." He stretched and reached into his jeans pocket and pulled out a joint. "But you, my friend, are getting fired anyway. So what have you got to lose? Care to indulge?" he asked with a wide grin.

Rick looked back at Randy with surprise. "How the fuck did you know that?"

"Know you were getting fired...? Don't get all uptight, Torrison. Rocelli didn't tell me anything, but it doesn't take a snowplow operator to figure you were gone with the flight cutbacks."

Randy lit up the joint and passed it to Rick. "Don't worry... I'm not going to tell."

For the next twenty minutes, the two men talked about the airport, Rocelli, and hunting, while slowly getting stoned. Sufficiently buzzed, Rick felt comfortable bringing the conversation back to the Stinson gold plane.

"You seen the Stinson Cessna this week, Randy?" he said with a big smile.

"Man, you are obsessed with that plane." Randy tried to stifle his own laugh. "I should tell you the next time it's coming in so you can get your fix!"

"Yeah, you do that." Rick laughed back at him.

"No...really...I can tell you."

"Tell me what?" Rick said, smiling and leaning back in the office chair.

"I know when it comes in...the day...the time... every week!"

Rick leaned the chair back to its upright position. "What do you mean...you know?" he asked, still chuckling.

"Well, can I trust ya, Ricky? Because, instead of the cops, I'll have to shoot you if I can't!" They both burst out laughing again.

"Okay...what is it?" Rick asked. "You buy a gold bar off the pilots every week?"

"Better...weed!" Randy said, still laughing.

Rick stopped laughing. "Weed? What the fuck are you talking about?"

"Yeah, the pilot, Fritz Rinestein." Randy tried to bring his own laughter under control. "He brings in whatever I need. Few ounces. One time in the summer, he brought me in half a pound. Sold most of it to the tree-planting crews."

Even with red eyes, Randy could see the disbelief on Rick's face. "Hey, those pilots don't make that much. And what better security than with a pilot who is greeted by the cops! Told you I was too smart for them, Rick!"

Despite his mellowed state, Rick was shocked at this information. He had to think fast.

"Hey, Randy...you need a partner? I can tell you I'm in a real jam with my mom and her hospital bills and I want to take her to Mexico at Christmas for a holiday. I bet I can use my Rennet Mine connections to sell a lot of weed."

"Ah, I don't know, Rick. I think Fritz would cut me off if he knew I even said anything to you. He's a pretty high-strung guy."

"Then don't tell him. Why does he have to know? You just tell him you've opened up new markets."

"And how would it even work? How could I trust you?" Randy asked, now staring back at Rick.

"Because I would give you twenty percent of everything I sell."

"Thirty!" Randy countered.

"Twenty-five!" Rick replied.

Randy sat back in his chair and stared at Rick with a glazed look. There was a long enough silence, and Rick wondered if Randy thought he had already said too much and was about to backtrack.

"Yeah, that might work," Randy said, bursting out laughing again.

He left Rick and did a half-hour check of the airport grounds before he came back to the Lake Fuels office. The two men took more time working out logistics. Randy explained that Fritz would tell him the month's schedule for flying into Tear Falls. He would then tell Randy to call him before the arrival of any flights and tell him how much weed he needed. When Fritz flew in, he would take the weed in his locked briefcase into the terminal while the Stinson mine workers loaded up the Cessna with the gold crates. Fritz would leave his briefcase in the baggage room, to which Randy had security access. Randy would walk in, open the combination lock on the briefcase, and exchange an envelope of money for the weed Fritz had brought in. The only thing that would change now was that Randy would give Rick a call to tell him when to expect a flight and to be ready for a handoff of his share. Both men agreed it seemed easy enough and shook hands on the deal, and then Rick left for home.

When he arrived, he saw it was 10 p.m. Still enough time to call Eduardo in Tijuana and give him some good news.

"Larga Vida Villa!" someone answered at the resort.

"Hola…hello," Rick said. "I was looking for Eduardo."

"Can I tell him who's calling?" the woman asked.

"Rick…Rick Torrison from Canada."

"One moment, please…"

As Rick waited, he could hear the woman talking to someone close by.

"Hey, Ricardo! You ready to book? Tell me you are coming!" Eduardo said loudly into the phone.

"I'm coming, my friend, but I'm doing things a little different this year."

"And how's that…dogsled?" Eduardo said, laughing.

"Nope…better, Eduardo. I have a plane now. Small plane I can fly all the way there," Rick replied

"Plane…? Hey, my friend, I know you fly the planes with the boat shoes, but there are no lakes here! Just a big ocean ready to swallow you up!"

Rick laughed. "I have a Cessna now, Eduardo. Part of a new business I am starting. It has two engines, wheels, and it can make it all the way to your doorstep. I don't need a lake. But I do need a landing strip near you. You have one?"

"You bring the plane, and I'll find you a place to land," Eduardo said. "You bring your mother on the same plane?"

"No, that is what I wanted to tell you. She is taking a regular plane. I'm going to have a nurse meet her at the airport. Take care of her until I get there a few days later. She doesn't like small planes, Eduardo. Is that okay?"

"Yeah…sure, Rick. But what day?"

"I'll have to phone you back. Most likely the third week of December. But don't worry if I have to pay for a few extra days. That's not a problem."

"Okay, Rick. I'm so glad you are coming, and happy for your mother, too!"

"Thanks, Eduardo. I will be back in touch. Adios!"

The next day, Rick visited the hospital at 10 a.m. and met with Dr. Siller in his office.

"Glad to see you, Rick. Please, have a seat," Dr. Siller said as he pointed to the chair in front of his desk. "Off work today?"

"Late shift today. Noon to eight," Rick replied. "Look, I'm sorry about the way I acted the other day at the meeting. It's just all this has been very stressful. Seeing my mother go downhill and all that."

"Understandable, Rick. So, what can I do for you?"

"Well, I thought I would talk to my mother and see if she would go to the nursing home for a few weeks on a trial basis before coming home. Actually, before we go to Mexico for our Christmas trip. You know, sort of part of her whole recovery so she tries it out without getting upset."

"Well, in the end, it's up to you and your mom, Rick. I can do the paperwork, and she can move to the nursing home by the end of the week. I like the idea." Dr. Siller reached into his desk, pulled out a piece of paper, and started making some notes.

"I do have one question for you," Rick said. "I'm thinking of taking her to a special clinic in Tijuana that treats MS."

Dr. Siller stopped writing and took off his glasses. "Rick, I know this hasn't been easy, but I would be cautious about throwing any money away on these promises of treatments and cures in places like Mexico. I can assure you, if something was working, we would have it here in Canada in one of our specialized city hospitals."

Rick was about to argue the point but thought better of it. He felt he had accomplished what he wanted to do in having his mother taken care of before they left. He didn't plan to return to Canada anyway.

"Yeah, I guess you are right. Warm waters and Mexican sunshine is probably just as good," he said, smiling.

Rick left Dr. Siller's office and went down to speak with his mom about their new plans. He told her she would be staying at the nursing home but only until they left for Mexico. He explained that she would take her own flight down and Eduardo would pick her up at the airport and make sure all her needs were taken care of. Rick made up the story that he was unsure of when his last day of work would be so he would be taking a last-minute flight to Mexico—which, by Rick's calculations, was entirely true.

Ricked looked at the office calendar and crossed off the twentieth of November. It had been over a week since he'd last spoken to Randy Biggs and they'd inked their pot-selling deal with a handshake. Randy had called the day before, so Rick was expecting him to stop by the Lake Fuels office at lunch.

Rick heard a familiar rap at the door, and he looked over and waved for Randy to come in.

"Hey, buddy. Man, it's f-u-c-king cold out there," Randy said as he removed his winter clothing.

"Winter does that, Randy. You got it?" Rick asked.

"Easy, Ricky. You lined up any sales?"

"I'm working on it, Randy. Takes a little while. Can't just call these guys up and say I've got some dope to sell. Have to ease my way into it, but I'll get there."

"Well, you better be working on it. I have to give Fritz fair warning." Randy reached into his back pocket and pulled out a small piece of paper. "Okay, here are the flight dates right up to Christmas. There is only one problem."

"What is it?" Rick asked, getting ready for a twist to his plans.

"The last flight…on December 22…it won't be Fritz. He's on holidays. It's going to be some rookie they have who just finished training."

Rick looked back at Randy with as much fake disappointment as he could muster.

"Fuck, Randy…are you kidding me! That's prime selling season! So, no dope on the twenty-second, then?"

"Hey, I can't control when the guy takes holidays, Rick. Fuck! Give me a break! Maybe we can bring in extra before that?"

Rick continued the charade, saying, "I don't know, Randy. Let's worry about that later. Show me the schedule."

Randy went over the other dates, but Rick was barely listening. He couldn't believe his good fortune of having a pilot unfamiliar with the routine of flying the Stinson gold plane in on the twenty-second. All he would have to do was tell Randy he still didn't have enough customers for Fritz to bring any extra weed for him to sell before that date.

Rick got home and went down to the basement to study Randy's list of flight dates and times. He took down a hanging calendar and circled the dates while writing the times. December 5, 1 p.m., December 12, 3 p.m., and December 22, 8 p.m. Working or not, Rick decided he would show up at the airport to test the truthfulness of Randy's dates.

Rick showed up for work for a noon-to-8 p.m. shift on December 5. He was relieved he didn't have to make up an excuse to hang out at the airport to make sure the Stinson gold plane came in on time. At 12:45 p.m., Rick watched out the office window as the familiar convoy of a van and police car pulled onto the tarmac. Within ten minutes the sight of a white and blue Cessna could be seen gliding in for a landing. He was sure Randy's flight information was now legit. His planning for his December 22 departure on the Stinson Mine gold plane could now begin in earnest.

The next day, he phoned Eduardo in Mexico. After settling December 19 as the day Rick's mother would fly down, Rick started talking about his own flight details.

"Eduardo, I should be flying in by early evening on the twenty-second. You got the airstrip for me?"

"Yeah, sure… It's called the Tijuana Airport!" Eduardo said with a laugh.

"No, Eduardo. I'm serious. I need an airstrip, not an airport. Somewhere close to you I can land. And it needs some lights. Something that can mark a runway at night."

"An airstrip? You are kidding me, right, Ricardo? Why do you need an airstrip? What are you bringing me? Smuggled polar bears?" Eduardo laughed again.

Rick lowered his voice, unsure of how Eduardo would respond to his next statement. "I'm bringing gold, Eduardo. Lots of it."

There was a brief pause before Eduardo said, "Gold…? I don't understand."

"I have been given gold to pay for my mom's MS treatment. Someone decided to help me out. But I can't bring it to Mexico the normal way. I need to bring it down on my plane and land somewhere out of the way that won't draw attention."

Again, there was a pause before Eduardo spoke. "I think… maybe I can help you, Ricardo. But this airstrip you need. It may cost you to land. That okay?"

"More than okay," Rick replied. "Just tell me how to find it."

Eduardo filled Rick in on the details of where he could find the airstrip on a map and some local landmarks that would guide him in even at night. Rick wrote everything down and told Eduardo he would call him back if he had any other concerns. The two men said goodbye, and Rick went to have a glass of rye. He swore when he saw the bottle was empty.

Rick came in on the early shift on December 10 at 7:30 a.m. The days were short enough now that it was dark at this time, and Rick was greeted by glowing multi-coloured Christmas lights Paul had strung around the office door. He came into the office and wrote a note to Paul requesting December 22 be his last day. He then changed and headed out for a 7:45 a.m. fuel-up.

Rick had just got into the cab of the fuel truck when the passenger door swung open.

"Hi, partner. Riding shotgun!" Randy said.

"Let me guess. Fuel security, right?" Rick said.

"You got it!" Randy replied. "Hey, last call for any orders there, partner. Next plane in two days. How are the new markets developing?"

Rick was ready to pull away, but he took his hand off the gear shift and turned to Randy. "They're not, Randy. Like I told you, it ain't easy to convince your friends you're now selling drugs. I'm thinking I might have to wait until after Christmas. I'll probably have more free time then anyway...wouldn't you say?"

"Just asking...just asking. No need to get all bent out of shape. Just saying Fritz needs to pay for the plane, too, you know?"

"Fritz owns the plane?" Rick asked.

"Yup. Owns four of them. His company is Brumen Air. It's in fine print on the side of his planes if you look close...real close!" Randy squinted his eyes at Rick. "He used to fuel up here, but Paul's old man got in a fight with him. Not sure what it was about, but Fritz said no more. He put in extra-large tanks and now flies round trip."

"Really...and how far do you think he flies?" Rick asked, once again welcoming Randy's valuable information.

"Well, I got to think it's near two thousand miles round trip, so you have to believe Fritz would make sure they can fly at least twenty-five hundred. All that just so he doesn't have to deal with Paul's dad anymore. Can you believe that? Two good businessmen who can't get along so both can make a buck. That's a serious disagreement!"

Rick agreed and then looked at his watch. "Well, I got to go, Randy. Sorry about the delay in orders. Will make it up to Fritz after the New Year." He put his hand back on the gear shift.

"That'd be good. See you, buddy." Randy jumped out of the truck, and Rick resumed his fuel rounds. He now knew why Paul never mentioned the Stinson gold plane and had made up the story about security when he had asked. He also knew there would be old invoices for Brumen Air somewhere in the office. Would there be any reason a rookie pilot would refuse a fuel-up if presented with the right paperwork?

Rick was not scheduled to work the next few days, so he took the time to visit his mom and get her plane ticket secured at the local travel agency. He also started packing. He placed four large suitcases out in the living room, two for clothes for his mom and himself and the other two for any mementos. There was nothing else in the house that could not be replaced, and since the home was rented from Rennet Mine for only a few more months, they would simply take it back and rent it to another mine worker.

Rick came back to work on the morning of the thirteenth. He was driving into the parking lot when he noticed Paul driving a fuel truck in the opposite direction. Paul pulled to a stop next to Rick and rolled down his window, and Rick did the same.

"Whole day on deliveries, Rick!" Paul said over the truck's idling engine. "Office is all yours. You'll see a light schedule. Looks like they have already cut one flight out per day! Oh, and by the way, I got your note about the twenty-second being your last day. Not a problem. Wish I could keep you on longer, Rick!"

"Yeah, would have been nice. Have enjoyed it!" Rick replied. "Hey, maybe we can have an espresso with some Sambuca in the coming days as a toast!"

"Now you're talking!" Paul said as he rolled up his window and gave Rick a wave.

Rick came into the office and saw his first fuel-up was at 10 a.m. He didn't waste any time searching for the old Brumen invoices. He pulled open a large file drawer and found folders labelled with government agencies, local gas stations, and private names, but nothing with the Brumen name. He was just about to close the drawer when he saw a file at the back labelled "Account Terminations." He took out the file and brought it back to the desk. He flipped open the folder, and the first name he saw was Brown Airways. The file was thick with a collection of unpaid invoices for Brown Airways and letters addressed to Pat Galverson demanding payment. Underneath the stack was a single paper with an invoice to Brumen Air. The stamp said paid, but there was a note below in handwriting that read "Account no good!" Rick took the invoice, folded it twice, and put it in his back pocket.

He took the next four days working routine shifts from 7:30 a.m. to 5 p.m. and using his nights to plan the details of December 22. Everything and everyone seemed to be cooperating except for one thing: Rick had no control over the weather, and a storm was expected for the twenty-second of December.

On the evening of the seventeenth, Rick sat in his living room, watching the 6:30 news for weather updates. Around him sat the four opened suitcases, three on the couch and one on an armchair. He also had various piles of clothes and items stacked around the living room, ready to be packed.

At 7 p.m., Rick heard the doorbell ring. He made an attempt to ignore it, but it rang again, and he heard the door open.

"Hello...Rick?"

"Yeah, right here... Is that you, Milt?"

Milt stuck his head around the corner. "Not surprised you didn't know it was me. You haven't heard my voice in so long, I bet you didn't even recognize it!"

"Hey, Milt. Yeah...been a while, hasn't it." Milt entered the room carrying a small package. "Here, let me clear a place for you to sit," Rick said as he moved items off a chair.

Milt sat down and placed the package he was carrying beside him. "And...?"

"Oh, sorry… Yeah…beer. One second." Rick went to the kitchen and returned with two beers. The two men toasted and drank.

"So, what's going on, Rick? Haven't heard from you in a month. No calls. Missed hunting season. And shit, look at your hair! You're getting worse than me!"

Rick reached up and felt the thick brown mop of hair on his head. "You know, you are right. Time for a cut, I guess." Rick got up from his chair. "You want a rye with that beer?" he asked, delaying his answer to Milt's question.

"Why not?" Milt replied.

Rick went into the liquor cabinet and remembered he was out of rye. "Shit" he whispered. He turned back to Milt. "How about a Scotch?"

"Wow! You must be busy. Rick Torrison without rye in the house!" Milt said with a smile. "Yeah, Scotch will work."

Rick filled two crystal glasses halfway with Scotch and went to the kitchen to get ice.

"You haven't answered my question," Milt yelled after him. "What have you been doing? Other than packing for a two-month vacation by the look of things."

Rick came back from the kitchen and handed Milt his drink. "Yeah, I know, Milt. I'm a deadbeat, but it's been busy as all hell. I had to move my mom to the nursing home. Rocelli always calls me at the last minute for any shifts, and now…get this… I'm being laid off in a week!"

Milt looked at Rick with a piercing stare. "And that's your excuse for not calling your best friend? I would think that would be more of the reason to call. You're a loser, Torrison!" Milt took a drink of his Scotch.

"Well, there is…another thing, Milt," Rick said, now taking his own large drink.

"Yeah…what's that? Rykin hired you back? Can't wait to hear this!"

"Not quite that good." Rick placed his drink down on the coffee table and looked directly at Milt. "I'm not coming back for a long time, Milt. A really long time! I'm going to stay in Mexico at least long enough to get my mom well. I'm going to bring her to that clinic I told you about. The one Eduardo talked about."

Milt raised his eyes to the ceiling. "Ah, man. Here we go! Now I know you've really lost it. C'mon, Rick! That shit is all talk. All talk for a clinic that wants to take your money. Your mom's money!" He got up from his chair and paced the room. "Your mom needs to be here, Rick. You need to be here. I haven't seen you in a fucking month! Kristen's been asking about you. Roddy's been asking." Milt walked back over to Rick and pointed his finger at him. "Tracy's been driving me nuts about you! Does none of that mean anything to you?"

"I've thought about all of that, Milt," Rick calmly replied. "That's how I know how important it is. But they aren't doing anything for her here. It's like...there's no hope. At least at this clinic, there is a chance. My mom deserves that chance."

Milt pursed his lips. "And how much? How much is this so-called chance going to cost you?"

"Well...Eduardo thought about twenty thousand...to start." Rick braced himself for Milt's response.

"Shit. And you think this is worth it? You really think they have some cure down there, Rick?"

"Look, I know it's a long shot. I know it costs money. I know I'm leaving a lot behind. But I have to do everything I can to try and beat this MS shit!"

Milt put his hands up in defense. "Okay...okay...take it easy. Don't start flipping out." He took a deep breath. "And what about the money? I suppose you are going to take Kristen and me up on the two thousand after all?"

"No, I've figured it out on my own. I will pay for it."

Milt looked back at Rick with surprise. "Really? Rocelli is paying you that much, is he? Or should I even ask about this one?"

"Probably not," Rick said finishing his Scotch. "Look, it's a done deal, Milt. My mom and I are going. It's going to work out, and we will be back in say…six months…six years. Who knows. Worry about that later."

Milt pushed his long black hair back with his hand and let out a sigh of frustration. "And how do you know this isn't a setup by your friend at the resort? Maybe this Eduardo is working with them. Some sort of scam. He might be getting a kickback on all this?"

"Thought of that, too, but he has known my mom and me for years now, and he has never brought it up. In fact, I was the one who approached him."

Milt sat back down. He leaned forward and put the palms of his hands together as though he were praying. "Well, it sounds like you have this all figured out, then. I don't think there is anything I can say now that is going to stop you. You going to keep in touch?"

"I will. One way or another."

"Well, I'm glad you are at least going to try to do that…one way or another."

"I think you will understand more once we get there, Milt. In fact, I think you will understand everything a lot more. At least, I hope you do."

"Okay, I can't pretend I know what you are going through or your mother. But you know me. I'm not a go-getter; I'm a go-better kind of guy. I will find something good in this no matter what. Like maybe Kristen and I and the kids will have to come and visit you to talk some sense into you to come home. After a week on the beach, of course."

"I knew you would come up with something."

"Ah shit, Rick, I guess I just wanted to make sure you have thought this all through. And at the very least that you know if it doesn't work out, we are here for you." Milt put his hands on the arms on his chair. "But I can see your mind is made up, and

I gotta go. You're still coming to the house for Christmas dinner, right? We can give you a proper send-off."

"Not going to miss that one for the world!" Rick replied as the two men got up from their chairs.

"If you need anything last minute, call me," Milt said. "Otherwise, send me a postcard and rub it in on how warm it is down there." He gave Rick a handshake and a hug. "Hope it all works out, my friend. For everyone!"

"It will," Rick replied. The two men walked to the door, where they shook hands again, and Milt left. Rick was closing the door when he remembered the package Milt had placed beside his chair. He pulled the door open. "Hey…Milt! What's in the package?"

"Open it! I'm just the delivery man! Talk soon, buddy!"

Rick came back into the living room, sat down in the chair where Milt had been sitting, and picked up the package from the floor. It was wrapped in a brown paper shopping bag and taped shut. He broke the tape and pulled out a note, which read: "Ricky! I kept thinking about what you said about your mother's bitch cramps from the fucking MS and went and got these from my aunt. Hope they help! Your friend Oakey. P.S. sorry that we both got fired." Rick opened the package further, and out fell a dozen hot water bottles. He carefully collected them, set them in a stack on his lap, and stared at them. He smiled at the thought that he would remember Oakey as a good person who was just trying to help and not for some fucked-up accident that had got them both fired.

Chapter Eleven

# SECURITY CHECK

Rick had a late-shift start of 12 p.m., so he visited his mom in the morning. He made sure she understood he would pick her up early the next morning for a 9 a.m. flight out of Tear Falls. He went over her connecting flight schedule and the arrangements he had made with both Eduardo and a nurse for her care until he arrived a few days later. Rick was pleased she was in good spirits, and even a little surprised to hear her say she would be more than happy to come back to the nursing home.

Rick arrived at the Lake Fuels office and could see Paul was over at the fuel tanks, talking to a delivery driver. He went into the office, turned on the radio, and listened for weather updates as he changed into his work clothes.

He didn't notice Paul come into the office.

"Hockey scores?" Paul asked.

"That, too," Rick replied, smiling. "Just trying to catch the weather for me...well, my mom...flying out tomorrow. You heard anything about a storm?"

"Not for tomorrow," Paul said. "Your last day maybe an easy one, though. Heard there could be a big one on Wednesday. I may even give you the day off with pay, Rick, if it's bad enough." Paul walked over and started preparing a small pot of espresso on the hot plate.

"Ah, you don't have to do that, Paul," Rick said, trying to hide his concern. "Even if it's snowing, I'll come in and sweep up. I'll find something to do. Always ready to earn my keep even on the last day!"

"Appreciate that, Rick. What day are you flying out again?"

"Thinking of the very next day. Maybe even the twenty-fourth if I can get a good deal."

"Nice," Paul said. "You might also want to get yourself a haircut before you go. You don't want them mistaking you for a drug dealer at customs."

"Yeah, I think my mother would say the same," Rick replied.

Paul took a hissing espresso pot off the hot plate and filled two foam cups. He grabbed a bottle of Sambuca from an overhead cupboard and poured a generous amount into each cup. "Merry Christmas, Rick! All the best with your trip to Mexico!"

"Merry Christmas, Paul!"

The next day, Rick picked up his mother at 7 a.m. and brought her to the Tear Falls Airport. He brought in the four suitcases he had packed and paid extra for their transport. After a kiss and a hug, he watched as staff took her out to the plane in a wheelchair and helped her board. He waved as the plane taxied out to the runway and took off. He turned to leave and ran right into Randy Biggs.

"Security check!" Randy said, pretending to pat Rick down and laughing. "Like my new security parka?" He turned around to show Rick the word "SECURITY" written in large block letters across the back of a bright yellow parka.

"Nice, Randy," Rick said. "You get a raise with that?"

"I wish! Guess they just wanted me to look more official. Make sure everyone knows that nothing is going to happen on my watch!" he said, smiling. "Like anything illegal...you know what I mean?"

"I hear you," Rick replied. Then, as the two men stared out the large terminal window at a clear day, he asked, "You think any flights will come in on Wednesday with the big storm coming? You think the Stinson Mine plane will take the chance?"

"Oh, it will be here," Randy replied.

"Because, I mean, if they didn't make it in, they will have to probably wait until after Christmas or something, right?"

"I suppose," Randy said, "but it has to be pretty bad for the plane not to come in for a scheduled pick-up." He turned to face Rick. "You have to remember, the plane is about money, not people. Nobody gives a shit about a few pilots risking their lives when you have a load of gold to go out. You would need one hell of a storm to stop that plane."

Rick laughed. "Yeah, I guess you're right. Forgot it is all about business. Even if it is a rookie flying the plane."

Randy looked at Rick with a creased brow, but then he smiled. "Hey, but stop worrying about a plane!" He slapped Rick on the side of his shoulder. "You're going south! When are you going to catch up with your mom in Mexico?"

"Next few days," Rick said. "Last-minute thing. Might even fly on Christmas if I get a deal! Which reminds me, I should go, Randy. Have the day off. Going to do my own packing." He turned and started walking towards the exit doors to the parking lot.

Randy watched Rick's back for a moment and then yelled out, "You have a good trip, Rick, if I don't see you! We'll talk when you get back!"

Rick turned around and backpedalled a few steps. He could see Randy was no longer smiling. "You got it. See you in the New Year!" He turned again and headed out to the parking lot.

He sat in his car and listened to the radio as he let the engine warm up. When he went to put the car into drive, he heard a loud pounding on the roof. He looked out the passenger window to see Randy looking in and asking him to unlock the door. Rick reached over and flipped the lock, and Randy got in.

"What's up, Randy?"

Randy took out a cigarette. "Push your cigarette lighter in!" he demanded.

Rick pushed the button in and waited for Randy to answer. "Randy...you upset about something? Do we really need to talk now? I'm busy—"

"Yeah, we need to talk! We need to talk right fucking now!" Randy turned to face Rick. "I want to know why you are so interested in a plane coming in that's not being flown by Fritz and that has no dope on it. What is it, Torrison? You not telling me something?" Randy jabbed his unlit cigarette at Rick. "If you are trying to fuck me out of something, it won't work!"

Rick had never seen Randy this angry. In fact, he had never seen Randy angry at all. "Why would I try and fuck you out of something? I haven't even done anything yet!"

Randy took the car lighter and lit his cigarette. "I don't know. Maybe twenty-five percent isn't enough for you? Money does funny things to people, especially when your mother is sick." He took a long drag on his cigarette.

"Randy, you need to calm down. You're getting all worked up for nothing. I just want to know how it all works so I don't make a slip-up. Didn't you say Fritz would freak if he knew you had a partner? Anything wrong with me trying to save my ass and yours?" Rick tried to sound indignant.

Randy looked back at him. "Fritz knows all about you, Torrison," he said with a smirk. "Do you really think I would be that stupid not to tell Fritz about a new person selling? He needed to check you out. We know all about your mom, the nursing home, and the bills. We even contacted the resort you are going to in Mexico and talked to your friend Eduardo. And by the way... how is that scar on your left arm healing?"

Rick looked back at Randy, trying his best to hide the shock at what he had just heard. He played along.

"Well, I guess it all checks out, then, right? Otherwise, we wouldn't still be here talking."

"Yeah, it checks out," Randy said, smiling. "Good for you that it does, because Fritz has a way of having people disappear who interfere with operations." Randy looked over and saw a blank look on Rick's face. He laughed. "Don't worry, Torrison... He's not going to kill you, although he probably would if he got mad enough. Let's just say he has the connections and the resources to have people lose their jobs. Sooner or later, those people move on, and like magic...poof...no more problem."

Randy opened the car door and stepped out. He looked back in at Rick. "We'll talk more when you get back."

He was closing the door when Rick yelled, "Hey, Randy! Did Fritz have anything to do with me losing my job with Rocelli?"

Randy looked back in. "Nope," he replied. "That was all legit. We even tried to keep you on. But like I said, Fritz and Rocelli don't get along." Randy looked in closer at Rick's face. "By the way, Rick, get a tan while you are down there. You're as white as ghost right now!"

Rick waited until Randy was out of sight. Then he opened his car door and threw up.

Rick got home and immediately tried to call Eduardo, but the front desk told him he had gone to run some errands and to the airport to pick up Rick's mother. He asked that Eduardo phone him as soon as possible. He hung up the phone and paced the house, trying to reassure himself everything was okay.

*Eduardo must have covered for me*, he thought. But he also thought maybe only Fritz knew the truth and hadn't told Randy. He was even starting to question the whole rookie pilot thing and thought he might be meeting face to face with Fritz Rinestein Wednesday night. He decided to go down to the basement and bring up two more long leather pouches for the trip. In one was his .306 hunting rifle, and in the other was a 12-gauge shotgun.

Rick spent the entire rest of the day checking on his maps in the basement and watching weather reports. He checked the duffle bag he was bringing three times and cleaned his guns four times. He was doing anything to pass the time as he waited for Eduardo to call.

At 4 p.m., the phone rang.

"Hello...Eduardo?"

"No, it's me...Paul."

"Oh...hi, Paul. How's it going?"

"Good. Listen, got an early Christmas present for you. Tomorrow's your last day. Like to give you the next two days off with pay. Maybe you can now join your mother sooner!"

"What...? Uuhh...yeah...no...no. I mean, you don't have to do that, Paul," Rick said, trying to switch his focus from waiting for Eduardo's call. "I can come in."

"No need, Rick. Like I told you before, I know what it's like to take care of a sick parent. My way of helping out."

"You've already done enough, Paul. I can—"

"Rick...stop arguing. It's my gift. It's not charity. Otherwise, I will have to fire you tomorrow and pay you anyway." Paul laughed. "Bring in your keys and ID tomorrow, and we will have one more drink...okay?"

"Got it, Paul. Thanks!"

"See you tomorrow."

Rick sat down in a chair and massaged his temples. He thought his head was going to explode.

At 7 p.m., the phone rang, waking Rick, who had fallen asleep in his chair. He jumped up and answered.

"Yeah...hello!"

"Ricardo! Everything is good. Your mother is here safe and sound!"

"Oh, that's good, Eduardo, but I need to ask you about something!"

"Easy, my friend. You sound out of breath. You are not running here, are you?" Eduardo asked with his familiar laugh.

"No...no!" Rick said, trying to bring his breathing under control. "Eduardo, did someone call you? Ask you about me? About my job?"

"Si…yeah. I would say…maybe two weeks ago… I don't know. He said he was your friend and wanted to get a room near you."

"Well, what did he ask? What did you tell him?"

"He asked when you were coming and how long you were staying. Why, Ricardo? You don't want this friend here?"

Rick declined to answer Eduardo's question. "Okay, but did you tell him I was coming down in my own plane. Like my new business. About the gold?"

"No…no. Is that what you are worried about? Ricardo, I may not speak your language, but I'm not stupid. I thought if he was a close friend of yours, he would know!"

Rick sat down in his chair. He felt a flush of relief flow through his body.

"Ricardo…you still there?"

"Yeah, I'm here, Eduardo."

"You are still coming, right? With the plane and everything and, like…the gold?"

"Yeah, I'm still coming. Gold and everything," Rick said, slowly rubbing the back of his head.

"Good. See you in a few days. And don't worry about your mom. She is happy to be in the sun!"

"That's great. Thanks. Hey, Eduardo…what was my friend's name who phoned?"

"Oh, he say his name was…like Milk…like you would put in your coffee? I don't know, but he didn't sound like you. He sound like he was from another country. Not Canada. You know him well…Milk?"

"I know a Milt, but I'm thinking it was someone different. Thanks, Eduardo. See you Wednesday night."

"You bet, amigo. Safe flight!"

Rick drove in Monday morning for his final shift at Lake Fuels. He still had a throbbing headache from the night before and his panicked discussion with Eduardo. He parked his car and took two aspirin from a bottle in the glove compartment. He took a deep breath, got out of his car and walked to the office. He was determined to convince Paul he needed to work the next few days. Within minutes of entering the office, he wouldn't have to.

As he walked in, he saw Paul with a big smile on his face, pouring himself a cup of espresso. He walked over and, without asking, poured himself a cup.

Paul looked at him, smiling. "I'll turn you into an Italian yet, Torrison!"

"Probably halfway there," Rick said, smiling back. He could see Paul was in an unusually good mood, and he decided to ask one more time to work for the next two days.

"Paul, about the next few days…"

"I know…I know…" Paul said as he put his arm around Rick's shoulder. "You have heard the rumours, and it's true. He'll be flying in on Wednesday. You can work that day. I know I will be dropping in!"

Rick stared at Paul with a confused look that Paul misinterpreted as surprise. "Hey, Rick. I'm a Stompin' Tom Connors fan as well. You'll get to meet him. Get your picture!"

Rick was stunned with the news. He struggled with his reply. "Yeah…well…thanks, Paul! That's exactly what I was going to ask you. I mean, I'm a big fan! Is he is still going to make it in with the big storm coming?"

"He'll fly in privately before noon. The storm's not expected to start until later in the afternoon. He has a place on Birch Island where he will spend Christmas. Whole family coming in, as I understand it."

"Great! Can't wait to meet him if I can!"

Paul finished his coffee. "Well, I'm off for more fuel deliveries in town. Take tomorrow off as planned, Rick. We'll see you Wednesday!"

Rick looked out the window as Paul got into a truck and drove away. He reached up to his head and noticed his headache had disappeared. *Stompin' Tom Connors. I need to shake your fucking hand*, he said to himself.

Chapter Twelve

# LEAVING IT ALL BEHIND

Rick woke up Tuesday morning to the doorbell ringing and someone knocking. He looked over at his alarm clock and was surprised to see it was 10 a.m. He realized he must have been more exhausted than he thought. He gave his head a shake. He would make sure he set the alarm for tomorrow morning. He got up with his grey sweatpants and his white muscle shirt on and made his way to the door.

He opened the door to see Tracy Rellis bundled up in a white parka, holding a gift basket wrapped in clear plastic.

"Hey, Tracy," he said. "C'mon in."

"Hey, sleepyhead," Tracy said with a big smile. She took her hood down, and her braided red hair shone brightly against her white parka. "Cold out there today."

"Yeah. What brings you here?"

"This!" Tracy said, handing Rick the wrapped gift basket. "Christmas present for you and your mom. You can enjoy it on the beach in Mexico if you want."

Rick took the basket and could see it was filled with cheeses, peanuts, and Christmas cookies. The top of a mickey of rye could be seen peeking out from the bottom.

"Made the cookies myself! Rest is from East End Grocers. Roddy added the rye."

"Thanks, Tracy. That's really nice of you," Rick said. "Hey, you want to come in? Coffee?"

"No…no. I work at eleven. Just wanted to say Merry Christmas. I know you have a lot of packing to do, and Milt said your trip might be for longer than usual."

"Oh, he said that, did he? Gotta love that guy!"

"He means well, Rick. I think he is worried about you. The stress and everything."

"I know, Tracy. I haven't been the best person to be around lately. But you know, it's going to all work out. I keep telling him that. Especially for my mom!"

"I know it will, Rick." Tracy reached into her pocket and pulled out a red Christmas card. "There is one more thing, and it's from Roddy and all of us at the NearNorth."

Rick took the card and looked over the red envelope. Snowflake, Santa, and snowman stickers surrounded the words "Rick and Mrs. Torrison" on the outside.

"What's this?" he asked.

"Open it," Tracy said. "Roddy wanted to be here, but he is being run off his feet with year-end orders and Christmas party preparations at the bar."

Rick opened the card and read the preprinted Christmas greeting. Around the outside were the signatures of Tracy, Roddy, and other employees from the NearNorth. Even Roddy's dad had signed the card. Inside was a cheque for two thousand dollars and a short note from Roddy. "Human mutual symbiosis is just another word for friendship. Merry Christmas, Rick!"

Rick looked at Tracy. "I can't… Tracy…this is too much. I mean, how? The bar is…"

"It's Christmas, Rick. That's all you have to know," Tracy said. "It's a gift, and we hope it brings you and your mom some relief from the worries of having to pay for her care."

Rick did his best to keep his composure. "You sure you don't want to come in? I mean, it will only take me a second to make some coffee…tea?" He looked back at the cheque. "I can't… This is unbelievable."

"No, I have to go," Tracy said.

Rick looked up to see Tracy staring at him. Her mouth was quivering in a closed-lipped smile. Her large green eyes strained to prevent tears from splashing down her face from a limbic system in emotional overdrive.

"It's going to be okay, Tracy," he said as he brushed his hand softly across her forehead and hair.

"I know it is, Rick," she replied. "It's just that…" She paused and closed her eyes, forcing a tear down her cheek. She leaned forward and gave Rick a kiss. "Just know we're here for you and your mom when you get back."

She put up her hood and turned to leave. "Give me a call." She took a few steps and, smiling, turned to correct herself. "I mean us."

"I will," Rick said, waving goodbye. "Tell Roddy thanks, and I will… I will call him…when I get back!"

"I will, Rick. Merry Christmas!"

"Merry Christmas, Tracy!"

For all the frenetic pace of the past few days, Tracy's visit was the first to give Rick some pause for thought. He walked into the kitchen, sat down, and contemplated what he was actually going to do tomorrow. He was going to steal a plane full of gold. He was going to fly to Mexico and land on a remote airstrip. He was going to take his mom to a clinic that wanted a twenty-thousand-dollar down payment. But most of all, he was likely leaving Milt, Tracy, and his friends and life in Canada forever. After some thought, he knew he didn't have much choice. He looked at his watch and decided to go to get his hair cut.

Rick woke up at 7 a.m. the next morning surprisingly relaxed. He made himself French toast and bacon and used his breakfast time to read over his Cessna manual. He took his coffee to the living room and turned on the TV. The forecast predicted light snow beginning around 4 p.m., but it was the wind that concerned Rick. It was predicted to be 20 mph at

6 p.m., but by 8 p.m., it was forecast to be 40 mph with gusts of up 60 mph. Would a rookie pilot fly a Cessna plane in under those conditions? And more importantly, would he be able to steal it and fly it out?

Chapter Thirteen

# FLY BY NIGHT

Rick arrived at the airport a little before 11 a.m. He parked and looked up through the windshield at a bright blue winter sky. Without the forecast, he would not have believed a major winter storm was on its way. He got out of the car and walked to the office through a near-full parking lot. All around him were travellers coming and going, but Rick had his head down, mentally going over his flight details.

"Hey…Rick!" Rick turned to see Paul calling to him out of the window of the company pickup truck. Paul drove around and stopped beside him.

"Whoa! New haircut and new leather jacket with the fleece lining, I see. And is that a new sweater? Wow. You must be ready for a picture with Stompin' Tom!" Paul said, laughing.

"Yeah. I thought I should be presentable." Rick laughed back. "It was about time I got cleaned up for customs in Mexico anyway."

"Good idea for Mexico," Paul said. His smile disappeared. "But bad news on Stompin' Tom, Rick. His plane is delayed until tomorrow. I know it looks good now, but they didn't want to take a chance. You want to take the rest of the day off and just come back tomorrow for a picture?"

"Really? Shit…that sucks, Paul." Rick looked up and squinted at the blue sky for time to think. "And no…no, I'm good to work the shift. Like I said, the least I can do for you, Paul."

"Okay. Your call. Not going to argue with a man that is looking so good. I'm going to town for my own shopping. Shouldn't be much happening here beyond three. Lock up anytime after that and slide the keys under the office door." Paul put the truck into gear. "And we'll have that drink after the picture tomorrow!"

"I'll be here!" Rick yelled out as Paul drove away.

Rick walked into the office and sat at the desk. He looked at the flight sheet in front of him to see only one fuel-up, scheduled for 2 p.m. He estimated he would be done with the fueling and all the paperwork by three. After that, there would be nothing more to do but wait for the Stinson plane at 8 p.m.

By 5:30 p.m., Rick found his morning calmness had all but evaporated. The early winter night made the airport dark, and Rick was nervously gauging the storm by the snow he could see blowing past the parking lot lights. The phone rang.

"Lake Fuels!"

"Rick! What are you still doing at work? Why aren't you here?"

"What do you mean? Why am I supposed to be there? I'm on a late shift!"

Rick could hear the phone being put down and picked up again.

"Richard Torrison! You get over here right now, and don't you disappoint your best friend for Christmas dinner!" Kristen yelled over the phone.

Rick sat on the edge of the desk and hung his head. "I forgot, Kristen. I forgot it was tonight. Shit!"

"Not a big deal," Kristen said, lowering her voice. "Simply close up when you can and come on over. We'll keep the food warm. We even invited Roddy and Tracy over!"

"Kristen...I can't. You guys go on without me. I'm going to be here until at least eight o'clock." Rick reached up and rubbed his short hair. He heard the phone switch hands.

"Hey! Fuckhead!" Milt said. "What's the idea of standing up your best friend, and worse, his wife!"

"I'm sorry, Milt. I know I'm a shithead. Just can't be tonight. What about a drink tomorrow?"

"You know Tracy has a thing for you," Milt replied.

Rick walked the length of the phone cord. "Milt, I can't deal with this right now. I can't deal with dinners, my mom, Tracy. It's all fucked up. I guess…I'm just sorry, buddy. I'm sorry for all of this, but I gotta go. I'll talk to you tomorrow." He hung up the phone.

He walked over to the window and stared out at the falling snow. He could feel his eyes starting to well up. "Ah, fuck it!" he said. He walked out to his car and retrieved the contents from the trunk.

He placed a hockey bag he used as his duffle bag on the top of the desk. The hockey bag was a gift from Milt, and it had a big Boston Bruins logo stamped on the outside. He unzipped it and began double-checking the items inside. In it, he had placed maps, money, food, and a crowbar. It also contained his rifle and shotgun. He took out the rifle and was checking the chamber when the phone rang again.

He was sure it was Milt, or even Tracy, phoning to convince him to change his mind. He let it ring five times before deciding to pick up.

"Yup!"

"Rick! It's nearly six o'clock! Go home!" Paul said.

"Oh…hi, Paul. Yeah, I was just leaving now. Just got caught up in the paperwork."

"Fuck, you scared the shit out of me! Ernie called from the terminal. He said there were lights on in the office and there seemed to be someone roaming around!"

"Sorry about that, Paul. Just lost track of time. I'll get out of here."

"Well, you should. Whole airport is shutting down in the next hour. May even stay closed for part of tomorrow."

"Next hour? But that is only seven o'clock!" Rick replied.

"Yeah…so? You seemed surprised. Care to take a look out the window, Rick?"

Rick realized the 8 p.m. Stinson plane had now been cancelled. A wave of cramps radiated up his back.

"Rick, if you're worried about tomorrow and Stompin' Tom… don't be! The airport will reopen tomorrow at some time. All is good. Go home and have a drink."

"Yeah…a drink. That would be good right now." Rick rubbed his face. "Thanks for calling, Paul."

"No problem." Paul paused for a moment. "Are you okay, Rick? You seemed pretty upbeat today. What happened? This all to do with missing Stompin' Tom?"

"No. Probably just… Well…I'm worried about my mom. I'll be okay, Paul. Thanks."

"Okay. See you at some point tomorrow. And just to let you know, Ernie asked Randy Biggs to check out the office. He may show his face there before you go. More than likely, he'll be stoned and useless as ever. Later, Rick!"

"Later, Paul."

Rick hung up the phone and slumped back into the office chair. He looked out the office door window and could clearly see Randy approaching in his bright yellow security parka. He jumped up, forced the .306 rifle back into the duffle bag, and threw it unzipped across the floor. It hit the wall with a thud, forcing a piece of the rifle stock out of the top. Just then, Randy knocked and walked straight in.

"Causing problems even on your last day, are you, Torrison?" Randy said as he pulled down his hood and unzipped his jacket.

Rick turned to face him and casually sat on the corner of the desk, doing his best to shield Randy's view of the rifle stock. "Hey, what did you expect, Randy? I like to go out with a bang!" he said with a smile.

"Figured that much," Randy said. He walked around the opposite side of the desk and went over to the window. "Nice little storm we got going here." He turned back to Rick. "So, why the late night?"

Rick could tell Randy's attitude toward him had changed since their conversation in the car. Gone was his easygoing manner. His questions were short, and his voice was full of suspicion. Rick not only figured he had lost his chance to steal the Stinson gold plane, but probably the fake drug deal he had with Randy as well.

"Paperwork. Just trying to get things in order before I'm out of a job. Leave Rocelli on a good note." Rick walked around his side of the desk and stood beside Randy at the window counter. He was still conscious of blocking the view of his bag to his right. He looked out the window. "Well, I guess a snowstorm can stop the Stinson plane after all. Can't say I blame them."

"Blame them for what?" Randy replied. "The plane will be here in twenty minutes. Half-hour to load, and the plane will be gone by seven. Why do you think they are shutting the airport down early?" Randy walked back over to the door. "What did I tell you, Torrison? The plane has no schedule. You better learn that before you come back if you want to work with me!"

Rick felt an uncontrolled shiver. "Hey, I'm a fast learner, Randy. I can adapt to anything. You'll see!"

"I hope so." Randy looked down to zip his parka back up. "You like the Boston Bruins, Torrison?"

"Ah...yeah. They're okay."

"I hate them. Don't put any drugs in that bag." Randy pointed at Rick's duffle bag. He put up his hood. "Get the fuck home. Wouldn't want to call the cops!"

"Yeah! I could do without that." Rick laughed as he let Randy out the door.

Rick waited until Randy had disappeared into the snow. He closed the door and rubbed his short hair with his hands to gather his thoughts. He still had a chance to make his plan work. He picked up the duffle bag from the floor, stuffed the gun stock back in, zipped it up, and placed it back on the desk.

He reached into his back pocket and took out his fake fuel P.O. order for Brumen Air with a shaking hand. He studied Fritz's forged signature and made sure the date and company number were correct. "All good," he said, breathing hard. His attention was immediately drawn from the paper to lights circling the office walls. He rushed over to the window and saw a van and an O.P.P cruiser drive through the airport gates and head for the loading area for the Stinson plane. At the same time, he watched as the navigation lights of a Cessna appeared through the snow and entered a glide path for a landing.

He went over to a cabinet and took out some truck keys. Then he put on his gloves and his Boston Bruins toque and grabbed the duffle bag. He was just about to go out the door when he went back to the desk and wrote Paul a note. "Sorry I missed Stompin' Tom! No hard feelings! Rick." He posted it on the bulletin board, turned off the lights, and headed for the truck.

He sat in the truck and waited. He needed to time this just right. He watched as the plane taxied and parked in position. He reached up, switched on the truck's airport lights, and started the drive through the blowing snow towards the parked plane.

He drove up and jumped out of the truck to a group of two pilots, four mine workers, and a provincial police officer, all staring at him and wondering what he was doing.

"Hi!" Rick said. "Bitch of a night to be flying ain't it?"

One of the pilots in a parka stepped forward. "What are you doing?" he said, shielding his eyes from the blowing snow.

"Here to gas you up!" Rick said, handing him his business card and pulling out his clipboard from underneath his arm. "If you can just sign here, I'll have you fueled up before these guys are finished loading. You can be on your way!"

The pilot turned to his co-pilot, and they started to talk out of Rick's hearing. The provincial police officer stepped forward to listen in on the conversation.

The pilot stepped back to Rick. "Let me see that clipboard."

Rick handed it to him with the fake paperwork. The pilot and the co-pilot looked it over using a small flashlight. There was some more discussion, and the pilot turned and handed the clipboard back to Rick.

"This can't be right. I was instructed to go round trip. There was never any mention of a fuel-up!"

Rick now knew this was the rookie pilot Randy had talked about. "Fritz phoned this in on a pre-signed form. That's his signature and the company right there, isn't it?" Rick pointed to the bottom of the form. "Fritz Rinestein? Brumen Air?"

The pilot took another look with his flashlight.

"Look, if you don't want to fuel up, I don't give a shit," Rick said over the wind, "but this storm is only going to get worse. You may not fly out tonight. You want to explain that one to Fritz?"

The pilot looked back at the workers standing around the van, waiting for his okay to load, and then up at the blowing snow. He looked back at Rick.

"Alright. Where do I sign? but you better be done by the time these guys finish. We need to get the hell out of here!"

Rick handed the pilot a pen. "Go in and grab a coffee. It won't take me long."

The pilot signed and signalled to the workers to begin loading. Rick watched for a moment as the pilots headed to the terminal and the police officer drove off. He immediately went around to start fueling the right side of the plane.

Within fifteen minutes, he was finished with the right fuel tanks, and he walked around to where the workers were loading on the left side of the plane.

"We're just about done," one of the workers, who appeared to be a supervisor, said.

Rick looked over at him and could see his eyebrows were crusted with snow. "No problem," he replied. "Don't want to get in your way."

Rick and the supervisor watched as the men loaded the last of the crates.

"That's it!" the supervisor said. "Go to it and get these poor bastards out of here. We're off!"

"Thanks," Rick said. "Oh...and...Merry Christmas!"

"Merry Christmas!" the supervisor yelled back, and then he and his crew jumped in the van and left.

Rick looked back at the terminal and could see the figures of the two pilots drinking coffee and looking out. He casually walked around the plane, got in the fuel truck, and manoeuvred it to the left side, essentially cutting off the pilots' view of the plane. He got out of the truck and fueled the left-side tanks.

He then carefully went over to the passenger side of the truck and opened the door. He took off his coveralls and threw them on the floor. Then he slid out his duffle bag and brought it to the cargo door of the plane. He reached up and pulled the latch.

*Shit...don't be locked*, he said to himself. The door fell open, and he could see the gold crates perfectly lined up on either side of the cargo hold. He threw in his duffle bag, climbed in, and closed the door. He made his way to the cockpit and sat in the pilot's seat. He took a moment to breathe, looking out the plane window. He could now see past the corner of the truck to the two pilots. They had been joined in conversation by a third person. He looked closer and could see it was Randy Biggs in his bright yellow parka.

"Hey, Mike! You made it in!" Randy said. "Not bad for a rookie run, there, pilot!"

"Fuck...look at you, Biggs! You look as stoned as you were on that fishing trip in the Bahamas!" Mike said.

"Have to make sure the merchandise is pure!" Randy said, laughing. He looked out onto the runway. "Hey, what's going on out there? That a fuel truck?"

"Ahh, Fritz ordered a fuel-up. I guess because of the storm. Not going to argue. I just wish he would hurry up. Want to get the fuck out of here before it gets any worse!"

Randy walked slowly to the edge of the window, concentrating on the Lake Fuel truck's flashing lights. "Fuel-up?" he said as he turned his head back to Mike. "The Stinson plane never needs a fuel-up. Who's driving that truck? Who said Fritz ordered this?"

"I don't know. This guy...Rick...Rick Torrison from Lake Fuels," Mike said, handing Rick's business card to Randy. "He had all the paperwork signed by Fritz. What? There a problem?"

Randy looked at the wrinkled Lake Fuels card with Rick's name half-smudged out. He then looked back out to the flashing truck. Despite being stoned, his eyes flew wide open. "Ooohhh... FUCK!"

Rick turned over the first engine and then the second. His hands and forehead were sweating despite the cold. He pushed the throttle levers forward and felt the Cessna lurch into motion. He slowly turned the plane to the right to begin the taxi out to the runway, and then he caught a glimpse of a running Randy Biggs in his bright yellow parka. Randy was frantically signalling across his throat for Rick to cut the engines.

Rick gave Randy a wave and smiled. He mouthed a message to him out the plane window: "Bye-bye, Randy. Fuck you!" Then he pushed the levers forward and left Randy standing in a backwash of snow.

Milt woke up the next morning still upset his best friend hadn't made it to their Christmas dinner. He had just turned on the radio for some Christmas music when the DJ interrupted for breaking news. He announced the Stinson gold plane had been stolen the night before from the Tear Falls Airport. Authorities confirmed it had crashed some forty miles outside of town. Milt went to pick up the phone to call Rick, and the receiver rang just as he touched it. He picked it up.

"Hello?"

"Milt. Milt Tonkin?"

"Yes."

"This is the Ontario Provincial Police."

Chapter Fourteen

# A NOVEL STORY

Milt sat in the window booth of the Abby Cafe, looking out over the parking lot. A ray of sunshine penetrated the window, giving him warmth even on a chilly April day. He was waiting for two other people to join him for lunch. An older-model red pickup truck drove up, and two men got out. Milt could see the back of the truck was filled with what looked like old camping gear, a bike, and probably a hockey bag or two. *At least they have a Boston Bruins sticker on the back windshield*, he thought.

The men came into the cafe and spotted Milt. They quickly brushed by other tables and marched directly toward him.

They spoke at the same time.

"Hi, Dad!"

"Hi, boys!" Milt said, giving each one of his sons a hug.

He looked at them with pride.

Nathan, his oldest, was now nineteen. He had Milt's straight black hair and had managed to outgrow his father by three inches, standing at six foot one.

His younger son, John, was eighteen. He was close to Milt's height of five foot ten and had the wavy brown hair of his mother.

Milt invited his two sons to sit down, and he handed them each a lunch menu. They sat for a moment in silence as they decided on their orders.

It was now 1984, and Milt had just turned forty-four years old. Gone was his long black hair, replaced by a thinner version neatly cut around his ears and squared off at the back. He had replaced his jean jacket with one of brown suede, and he wore wire-rimmed bifocals as a mandatory part of his day.

When the waitress came over, John recognized her from his grade-twelve class. "Hey, Janice!" he said.

"Hi, J.T.!" Janice replied. "You guys ready to order?"

Milt said, "Well, I don't care what you boys order, but we are all getting a chocolate milkshake made the original way, with scoops of ice cream and the mixer. None of this out-of-the-machine crap! And put me down for a grilled cheese and fries, please."

"Hey, I'm up for that, Dad," Nathan said. "And I'll have the double cheeseburger and fries!"

"I'm going for the Abby Burger, Janice," John said. "And…an order of…onion rings, please!"

"Got it," Janice said as she finished writing everything down on her order pad. "Be right back with the milkshakes!"

Milt turned to his two sons. "So, what brings me the pleasure of a lunch with my two busy boys on a Saturday afternoon? Other than me paying, of course."

"Well, we have something to ask you, Dad," John said. "It's like…well…we are thinking of going on a camping trip. You know, like we do with you on hunting trips or the way you used to do with Uncle Rick."

"Why do I think I'm not going to like this? We are not even close to hunting season," Milt said. "C'mon, spit it out. What are you two boys up to?"

"Tell him, Nathan," John said.

Nathan reached into his back pocket, pulled out a worn paperback, and threw it on the table. "That might be the best way to explain it, Dad."

Milt looked down at the book and then back up to his two sons. "No! Absolutely not! Are you two crazy? Throw that book out!"

Janice interrupted the conversation by bringing the chocolate milkshakes to the table. In front each man, she placed a tall, old-style glass of milkshake with a straw standing straight up in the middle.

"Hey," she said, "is that the book on the Torrison treasure?" She picked the book up off the table. "My dad read this. He thinks the gold is still out there!" She looked around the table with a smile, but she was met with three blank stares.

"Yes, there was gold out there, young lady," Milt said, "but there is nothing there now. It's all been found. Now, can you check on our food order, please?"

Janice put the book down, shrugged, and walked back to the kitchen.

"Dad!" John said. "She was just asking!"

Milt picked up the book and shook it at John and Nathan. "This, boys, is just some garbage asshole author from down south trying to make a buck off of my dead friend. There is no gold out there. The Stinson Mine recovered every bar!" He slapped the book back down on the table.

Both boys sighed and sat back in the booth. Nathan looked at his dad and did his best to be soft-spoken. "That's not what the book says, Dad."

Milt took a sip of his milkshake and shook his head. "Okay. I read the book when it came out six years ago. Give me the evidence. And you know your dad! I can spin anything into a positive. So, I'm all ears!"

John and Nathan looked at one another and couldn't believe they had even made it this far with their dad.

*The Torrison Treasure* was a book written by a man named Chris Berts, a newspaper reporter from Southern Ontario. He doubted the official 1971 report surrounding the crash of the Stinson Mine gold plane and believed there was a cover-up. It took authorities three days to find the white Cessna Rick had crashed on a snow-covered lake forty-one miles northwest of Tear Falls. Police reported recovering Rick's body and the gold. Yet a trapper who tipped off the police on the plane's whereabouts reported seeing no gold at the crash site. Rumours swirled that the Stinson Mine was deliberately misleading people. The author argued the gold was never recovered by the mine, and all sorts of theories followed on how it might have exited the plane.

John flipped to a dog-eared page in the book and showed his dad. "See, Dad. Berts says Uncle Rick had never flown a Cessna before. He may not have secured the latch on the cargo door right, and the gold could have slid out when he was over Yars Lake."

"Or maybe he pushed it out when he knew he was in trouble! Berts says Uncle Rick had paratrooper training from the army. He would have known how things fall out of planes!" Nathan added. "He says that in another part of the book where the trapper that found the plane heard the plane circling!"

"Okay," Milt said, "let's say either one is true. Anything can make sense if you are trying to make a buck like this Berts guy is trying to do. Bottom line is it makes no sense that the Stinson Mine would say they found the gold when they didn't."

Janice returned with three plates of food and put them in front of the men. "Here you go, J.T., Nathan!" she said, smiling. She placed Milt's food in front of him and said nothing.

"They didn't want people treasure hunting, Dad!" John said. "It was bad for their reputation and business. Berts talks about how they came back in the spring, saying they were cleaning up the site. They had a ten-man crew there for four weeks! All to pick up some missing airplane parts?"

"Well, I guess you boys are right, then," Milt said with a mouthful of grilled cheese. "It's there, somewhere. Scattered across God knows how many miles of bush." He took another drink of his milkshake.

"I don't believe it, but go ahead and look. Even if it's not there, it's a great opportunity to gain some camping experience. I say go for it! When is this so-called prospecting trip planned?"

"May long weekend!" the two boys said in unison.

When Milt arrived home, he sat on the couch and picked up a magazine. He was still digesting the Abby Cafe lunch as well as his two sons' plans to travel forty miles up a logging road and camp for a few days in search of some legendary gold. He'd been truthful with them in expressing his reservations. But he'd lied about reading the book only once when it came out. He'd read it five times.

"Hey, how did the lunch go with your two boys?" Kristen said as she sat down beside him.

"Good. But get ready for a request you are not going to like when they get home!"

"Oh, about their trip to find Rick's gold?" Kristen rubbed his short hair.

"You knew? And you approve?"

"They're adults now, Milt. Young, yes, but they already know how to take care of themselves in the woods. You taught them as much on the hunting trips you've taken them on." Kristen looked into his eyes. "What are you worried about?"

Milt sat back and exhaled. "I don't know. I always try and be the optimist, but I guess I'm still angry about the whole thing. I'm angry that I'm angry. Tell me, Kristen, why didn't Rick just come to us? We could have taken out a loan to help him and his mom even if it was a crazy idea!"

"That answer hasn't changed, Milt. Rick was all about his pride and his mother. He couldn't look beyond that. You know that as well as anybody." Kristen stood up. "Which reminds me. Oakey called. He is going over to see Rick's mother at the nursing home this afternoon if you want to join him. He said Dr. Siller is talking about her needing an electric wheelchair soon."

"That's another thing," Milt said, standing up. "His mom is still alive, and guess what? She's doing alright. How screwed up is that, Kristen!"

"Milt, we've been over this. Have a beer. Go see Rick's mom. Go see Oakey. You will feel better." Kristen turned and walked back to the kitchen.

Milt drove to the Tear Falls nursing home. As he entered the lobby, he saw Oakey on the way out.

"Milty! How's the new Rennet Mine union rep?" Oakey said, putting an arm around Milt's shoulder.

"Couldn't be better, Oakey. How's she doing?"

"She's doing fine, but she's resting. Bought her a new pillow. I would let her sleep, Milty. Want to grab a coffee in the cafeteria?"

"Sure, why not."

Milt found a table in the cafeteria while Oakey went over to buy two coffees. The two men had become good friends ever since Rick's death, and Milt was glad they now shared the common commitment of taking care of his mother.

Oakey brought back Milt a foam cup of coffee but had decided on a Coke for himself.

"So, how do you like driving a logging truck, Oakey?" Milt said, stirring his coffee.

"Suits me just fine." Oakey cracked his can of pop open with a loud hiss. "Gotta watch that the load doesn't shift on tight corners. But most of the time, I just listen to the radio and drive."

"Oakey...how many times have you read the Torrison treasure book?"

"Enough to make me want to strangle that Berts guy. Why?" Oakey asked, taking a big drink of his Coke.

"You believe the gold is still up there? All this shit the guy wrote in the book about a Stinson Mine cover-up?"

"Who knows. I'm more interested in what happened to that security guard who went missing a week later."

"You mean that Biggs guy? That guy that drowned ice fishing?"

Oakey looked at Milt with a crooked smile. "Milty, the newspaper said he got drunk and walked off and fell through some thin ice on Fenny Lake!"

"Yeah…so?"

Oakey took another drink of his Coke, emptying the can. He leaned in close to Milt and his voice went low. "There ain't no thin ice on Fenny Lake! I've ice fished there myself. There ain't no currents, no open water, and no thin ice unless you are an elephant."

Milt leaned back in his plastic cafeteria chair, rubbing his fingers over the side of his foam cup. "Okay, now you're screwing with my head, Oakey. You've never told me this. You think the guy was purposely killed? Like murdered?"

"Don't know. None of my business. But he was there with the DeMello twins and one other guy. Maybe they were drunk. Maybe there was an accident. But it wasn't wandering off and falling through thin ice. Big bullshit there!" Oakey looked back over at the food counter. "Think I'm going to get a piece of pie. Want one?"

"No…no thanks, Oakey. I'm going to head back home." Milt stood up, finished his coffee, and threw the cup in a nearby garbage can. "Thanks for buying Rick's mom the pillow."

"Sure thing!" Oakey said. "I will call you for some four-wheeling when it dries up!"

Milt gave Oakey a wave goodbye, headed out to his truck, and started his drive home. He was far from feeling better; Oakey had just given him one more thing to think about. As the new Rennet Mine union rep, Milt was constantly encouraging members to take advantage of the counselling service. He was now starting to think he should do the same.

Chapter Fifteen

# COUNSELLING

J ohn rotated the numbers on his combination lock and pulled. The lock clicked, and he pulled out the gym locker drawer containing his street clothes. He placed the drawer on the bench and sat down to remove his shoes and gym uniform.

He looked up to see Mr. Strott, his grade-twelve gym teacher, enter the locker room. He was wearing his usual tight short-sleeved pocketed gym shirt and striped long gym pants. "Going to hand out the health tests before you go!" he said.

Gerald Strott was a teacher who thought the best way to toughen up his students was to tell it like it is. He called it his "no bullshit rule." If you messed up, you were going to hear about it, and most often, this took the form of him ridiculing you in front of the class. Nowhere did he do this better than when giving back tests to his students.

Strott went around the room, passing out the tests and announcing the marks for all to hear.

"Kyle! Fifty-six. Good enough for a school bus driver, but that's it, Kyle!"

"Lance! Thirty-eight. Yeah. Going places, Lance!"

"Chad! Seventy-one. Good for playing hockey and living in the bush!"

"John! Ninety-four. Now, that's how it's done!"

Strott finished giving out the tests to the rest of the students. Everyone received their personal commentary and just accepted it as part of being in his class.

Chad DeMello stood up to button his shirt and looked down at John's test on the bench beside him. John's mark of ninety-four percent was circled in red with an "Excellent" comment from Strott at the top. "What's with you, Tonkin?" he said. "You have a photographic memory or something? You play just as much hockey as I do!"

Chad DeMello was the same age as John, and they both played in the local hockey leagues. Chad had taken after his dad in being a tough, hard-hitting player, and he had inherited his father's willingness to fight. He was also a big hunter and fisherman and would often brag at school about having survived long days out in the woods with nothing more than a gun and fishing rod.

"Ah, just luck, Chad. And a few coloured pencils," John said. "I write different notes in different colours so when I have to remember something, I just remember the colour, and everything comes back!"

John pushed his locker drawer toward Chad so that he could see the pack of coloured pencils inside. "Go ahead. Take these. I've got lots at home."

Chad reached into the basket but bypassed the pencils and pulled out a book. "What the fuck's this? You reading *The Torrison Treasure*?"

"It's a good book! May do a book report on it," John said. He stood up and put out his hand for Chad to return the book.

"Your dad was friends with that guy, right? The guy who stole the gold?" Chad said as he held the book close to his chest.

"Yeah, they were good friends!" John replied. He already anticipated Chad's next question. "But my dad knew nothing about him stealing a plane full of gold!"

"I find that hard to believe," Chad said, throwing the book back in John's basket. He placed his own locker drawer back and picked up his textbooks off the bench. "My father and my uncle have been looking for that gold for years. Maybe they should just call your dad!"

The end-of-school bell rang, and Chad turned and walked out of the room.

John placed his own locker drawer back and ran out to the parking lot to catch his ride home with his brother. He got into Nathan's pickup truck and threw his textbooks on the seat beside him.

"You know you don't have to rush. We don't have a hockey practice this afternoon," Nathan said, starting the truck and driving out of the parking lot.

"Yeah, I know," John said, catching his breath. "You know Chad DeMello's dad and uncle have been looking for the gold from the plane? That means we're not the only ones who think it's out there!"

Nathan leaned over and turned on the radio. "Yeah, how do you know that?"

"Chad saw the book in my gym locker. He said dad should know where it is, being Uncle Rick's good friend."

Nathan looked back to John with surprise. "You didn't tell him we were going to look for it, did you?"

"Nope. Told him I was reading it for a book report," John replied.

"Good! Because all we need is for Chad to be spreading that rumour around school."

John looked out the window and then back at Nathan. "Do you think Dad does know more than he is telling us?"

"Like what?" Nathan asked.

"I don't know. He just hates talking about Uncle Rick's death. Even after all these years."

"I wouldn't worry about it. He is letting us go. That's more than I would have ever expected from Dad. I think he just gets angry that the whole story never seems to go away."

"Yeah, maybe," John said.

Nathan turned up the radio, and the two boys sat in silence the rest of the way home.

That evening, Milt sat down at the dinner table and looked over his plate. "Ah...meatloaf, my favourite!"

Kristen poured everyone milk to drink and sat down, with Nathan and John on either side of her and Milt at the end of the table.

"How was everyone's day at school?" she asked.

"All the same, Mom," Nathan said. "Lots of projects due. Teacher's trying to cram as much into grade thirteen as they can!"

"Got my health test back," John said. "Ninety-four percent!"

"Grade twelve is easy!" Nathan replied, smiling at John.

"Pretty good just the same," Milt said.

"Dad, how well do you know Chad DeMello's father?" John asked.

Nathan frowned at his brother.

"You mean Marty DeMello?" said Milt.

"Yeah," John replied.

"Can't say I know him very well and can't say I would like to. The two brothers have always been trouble in Tear Falls, and as I hear it, the son is not far behind."

"Why are you asking, John?" Kristen asked.

"He saw I was reading *The Torrison Treasure* and said his dad and uncle have been searching for it for years," John said. "He seems to think just because Dad knew Uncle Rick that Dad knows something more about where the gold is."

Nathan narrowed his eyes at John. "Why did you have to bring that up?" he whispered.

Milt put down his knife and fork and placed his hands on the table. "Okay, was it not good enough that I said you boys could go on your trip? Now you are talking to the DeMello kid about it!"

"I didn't say..."

"It doesn't matter what you said. Chad DeMello, his dad, and the whole DeMello family attract trouble. Stay away from them, period!"

Milt picked up his fork and began eating to a silent table. Nathan looked at John and shook his head.

Nathan and John retreated to their rooms after dinner, while Milt took a beer into the living room to watch TV. Kristen came in with a glass of white wine and sat in an armchair near Milt, who was on the couch.

"They know enough to stay away from the DeMellos, Milt. You don't have to take your anger for Rick out on the boys," Kristen said.

Milt sat up on the couch. "I'm not worried about the boys staying away from the DeMellos. I'm worried about the DeMellos staying away from the boys. There's a difference!"

"I'm not sure what you mean by that," Kristen replied.

Milt picked up his beer off the coffee table. "If the DeMellos know the boys are going to look for the gold, they're going to think the boys know something. They know the connection between me and Rick. Shit, even the cops questioned me for two years after the crash about Rick's plans to steal the gold!"

"Milt, I think you are taking this whole bad DeMello twins thing too far. Sure they get into a few fights, and Marty's kid is not the best, but I hardly see the boys in danger even if they do know they are going to look for the gold."

Milt rubbed the bridge of his nose with his thumb and index finger. He looked up. "You know what Oakey told me the other day? Remember that airport security guy who went missing around the same time Rick had the plane crash?"

"Yes, I remember him perfectly. Randy Biggs. He died in the ice fishing accident. His mother still works over at East End Grocers."

"Yeah, well, Oakey doesn't think that was an accident. He thinks something else happened. And guess who else was there? Both DeMello twins."

Kristen leaned forward in her chair, her glass of wine cupped between her hands. "So, what exactly is Oakey saying? The

DeMellos had something to do with his death? That it was not an accident?"

"I don't know, Kristen," Milt said, looking directly at her. "That's exactly the problem. He didn't really say. He just said the story of him falling through thin ice was bullshit. And if anybody knows the ice on Fenny Lake, it's Oakey!"

Kristen took a sip of her wine. She rested her elbow on the chair, placed her right hand to her cheek, and stared at Milt.

"I'm sorry, hon," Milt said. "I'm not trying to scare you. It was over thirteen years ago, and I'm sure the police did a proper investigation. It's probably just all my own insecurities with my friendship with Rick coming back."

Milt finished his beer and stood up. He clasped his hands on the top of his head and looked out the living room window.

"Milt, I know I have asked you this before, but do you think the gold is still up there? Do you have any doubt about the police report and what the Stinson Mine said about recovering it?"

Milt turned around. "Yes, I believe every word of it, Kristen. Every last fucking word, in fact. Nothing else makes sense."

"Because sometimes you don't act like it. Sometimes I wonder why you get so upset when someone says otherwise."

Milt walked back and sat down on the edge of the couch. "Kristen, do you remember what that Chris Berts guy said when he came here to ask me questions for his book?"

"Yeah. He was an asshole. He said he could turn Tear Falls—"

"Into the next Oak Island!" Milt finished. "He could make me famous, you famous…the whole fucking area famous. He didn't give two shits that Rick was dead. About his story of trying to help his mother. It was all about him and what he wanted to write, not what he heard."

"I understand all that, Milt, but what do you truly believe? Who is telling the truth?"

"I believe the authorities. The police and the Stinson Mine. Is that not who you are supposed to believe? And why not? It keeps my mind on everything that is important. That Rick was a good friend, a good uncle to our kids, and a good son trying to help his mother. It's what he would have expected me to believe, and that's what is important."

"Then I believe it too, Milt," Kristen replied. "I love you."

Milt leaned over and pressed his forehead to Kristen's. "I love you, too." He kissed her and stood up. "I think I need another beer. And maybe I need to go to the mine counselling program like I tell my union members."

"That might not be a bad idea. Maybe we can go as a couple."

Chapter Sixteen

# RADIUS

At lunch, Nathan met John in the school library, where they signed out a study room. John went to the geography section of the library to retrieve some maps of the local area while Nathan took out *The Torrison Treasure* and flipped to some marked pages.

John came back into the room with a map and unrolled it on the table. He placed textbooks on the corners to keep it flat and pulled out a protractor with a pencil.

"Here is where the plane crashed on Yars Lake, and here..." John placed the protractor pin on the lake and swung the pencil in a circle marking a three-mile radius. "...is how Uncle Rick would have circled from what it says in the book."

Nathan took out a piece of paper, wrote down some numbers, and punched them into his calculator.

"That works out to almost thirty square miles!" he said, sitting in his chair and hanging his head back. "Thirty fucking square miles of Northern Ontario bush! Dad was right. That could be a needle in a haystack even if it is true!"

John suddenly pushed Nathan forward and below the table.

"What the hell are you doing?" Nathan said as John joined him.

"Chad DeMello!" John said. "Just saw him walking by the window!"

The two boys poked their heads up to see Chad and a friend walk backwards and look in. Chad opened the study room door.

"The Tonkins! Always studying!" Chad said. "You guys should be playing Space Invaders with us on the computer next door! Now, that's fun! Not this shit." Chad nodded at the map.

Chad came around the table and purposely nudged Nathan and John out of the way to get a closer look.

"What the fuck is this?" he said, pointing to the pencil circle around Yars Lake.

"Nothing," John said, looking at Nathan for support.

"Geography assignment!" Nathan said.

Chad looked at the side of the map and saw the Torrison treasure book.

"Bullshit!" he said. He looked at his friend with a smile. "I think what we got going on here is a little Torrison treasure hunting!" Chad's friend smiled and nodded in agreement.

Chad picked up the book and flipped through some of the marked pages. "Why do you waste your time on what this guy says?" He gazed back at the map. "And is that circle supposed to be a search area?" He laughed. "Shit. Might as well bring in the Canadian army!"

He threw the book on the table and walked back to the door. He turned around. "Good luck, losers! Better yet, why don't you ask your dad where the gold is before you go. He'll save you some time!"

He left the room, followed by his friend, and gave both boys a smile and a wave through the window as he left the library.

"That guy is a nutcase," Nathan said.

"This is not good," John replied.

"What is not good?"

"Chad is going to go back to his dad and tell him we're looking for the gold. Chad is convinced we know something more than we are telling because of Dad."

Nathan rolled up the map. "Don't start with that again. Who gives a shit what Chad's dad or his uncle thinks, even if they do know. Let them look for themselves!" He picked up his textbooks and handed John the map. "We can talk more about this at home. See you after school!"

Nathan left for his next class, and John returned the map to the geography section of the library. He was bothered by Chad DeMello, but not because he knew they might be looking for the gold. He was starting to wonder whether Chad was right. Did his dad know something more about the Torrison gold that he was unwilling to tell even his own sons?

\*\*\*

At the East End Grocers, Kristen walked in, said hi to one of the cashiers, and went straight to the butcher's counter.

"Hi, Josh!" she said with a smile. "Got my steaks ready to go?"

Josh Rula took out a package of steaks wrapped in brown paper from a cooler behind him.

"Let me see…." he said as he put his ear to the package. "Nope…they say they aren't ready. Guess you will have to come back tomorrow!"

Kristen smiled as Josh handed her the steaks. "That new Super Mart store opening down the street doesn't worry you at all, Josh?"

"Not at all!" he said. "We have better jokes!"

Kristen laughed. As she turned to approach the cash register, she noticed Carol Biggs sitting at a table at the back of the store, drinking a coffee. She decided to go the other way and walked back towards her.

"Hi, Carol!"

"Oh, hi, Kristen! How are you?"

"I'm good. On break?"

"Yeah, ten minutes to give my feet a rest," Carol said, reaching down and rubbing her ankles.

"Your boss there doesn't seem to be much worried about the new store opening up," Kristen said. "That's good!"

"Yeah. Josh never worries. Or at least, he doesn't tell us." Carol smiled.

Kristen tapped her fingers on the chair back in front of her, searching for something more to say. "Mind if I sit down?"

"Sure. Want a coffee?"

"No thank you." Kristen placed her wrapped steaks and purse on the table. "Carol, I don't want to bring anything up you don't want to talk about, but we share some of the same tragedy in that our best friend Rick died around the same time your son passed away thirteen years ago."

Carol's demeanour darkened. "It might have been the same time, but I see things a little differently."

"Oh!" Kristen said with surprise. "Why is that?"

"Your friend stole a plane full of gold right from under my son's nose. Wasn't like he didn't know what he was doing. My son was just trying to enjoy life ice fishing. And whose death gets all the attention from the cops, your friend, the criminal."

Kristen could tell she had made a mistake, and she stood up to leave. "I'm sorry," she said. "Stupid of me to even bring it up. I'm sorry for your loss."

Carol took a sip of her coffee and looked back up at Kristen. "Why did you bring it up, then? Why are you talking about my son's death thirteen years later?"

Kristen let out a breath. She was unsure whether she should say anything more. "Well, you mentioned the cops. Do you think they did a proper investigation of your son's death? Do you think they did their job? Because I don't know if they are even telling the truth about our friend Rick's death and this whole stupid gold story!"

Carol stared back at Kristen, deciding on her options. "Sit down," she finally said, and then she whispered, "I never believed any of it. My son did not drink. Sure, he smoked weed once in a while, but that was it." Kristen could see Carol's foam coffee cup bending under her grip. "And you know what the cops said when they pulled my son out of the water with bruises and cuts? That they can happen to anyone struggling in icy water!"

Kristen felt her breathing become shallow. "What happened when you told them you didn't believe it, that he fell through the ice and didn't even drink?"

"Nothing," Carol said, sitting back and finishing her coffee. "They said there is a first time for everything. They weren't going to worry about a young, pot-smoking kid. Besides, my son was there with the cops' best buddy, Fritz Rinestein. He's the guy who owned the plane your friend crashed."

"I thought it was the DeMello twins who were there," Kristen replied.

"Oh, they were there, too, but they just follow Fritz's orders. They do whatever he says... Still do!"

Kristen bit her lip. "Carol, I don't know what to say. So, you think this Fritz and the DeMellos were responsible for Randy's death?"

Carol placed her empty cup on the table. "I always thought that. I think Fritz caused my son to have an accident. I think he was pissed that his precious little plane was stolen, and I think he blamed Randy for the whole thing." She looked up at the wall clock and then back to Kristen. "But that's just me. I can't go up against a guy like Fritz Rinestein, with all his friends. He seems to have his hand in everyone's pocket, or theirs in his!"

Kristen placed a hand on Carol's. "Is there something that we can do now? Can I help you in going back to the police?"

"No. Fritz is still around, and that means the police are probably still his pals. And I know, no matter what Josh says, I need this job even if I have to go over and work at the new Super Mart myself. Last thing I need in my life is to have my name in the paper."

Both women turned to the sound of Josh Rula's voice. "Sorry, Carol, but I need you to help out in the back stockroom."

Carol stood up. "I have to go. I'm sorry about your friend. I actually remember Randy talking about him. Good luck finding out anything from the cops, though!"

Kristen watched as Carol disappeared into the back of the store.

She stood and walked slowly to the store exit, trying to catch another glimpse of Carol to make sure she was alright. She was consumed with everything Carol had told her. She was about to leave the store when she heard a voice.

"Ma'am...ma'am!" the cashier yelled out. "You have to pay for those steaks!"

Kristen arrived home at the same time Milt was walking up the driveway from the mine bus stop.

Milt waited for her to get out of the car. "Hi, hon!" he said.

"Hi," she said, walking right by him. She turned. "Do you want to go to the NearNorth for a drink after dinner?"

"Sure...I guess... What?"

***

Milt and Kristen walked into the NearNorth bar at 8 p.m. and stood at the front door. It was relatively quiet on a Tuesday night, but they were already feeling uncomfortable and out of place. They both scanned the room and were lucky to see anyone they could guess was over twenty-five years of age. Kristen looked at Milt.

"Maybe we should just go to the Abby for a coffee," she said.

"I don't think we have a choice now," Milt said, pointing to a smiling Roddy Simone coming their way.

"Hey, love birds!" Roddy said, giving Milt a hard handshake and Kristen a big hug. "What brings you two to my fine establishment? I know it's not this new generation of music I have to play on the jukebox now. The Spoons... We talking music or soup, Milt?" He laughed.

"I'm with you on that, Roddy. Beer is always good for me, thanks," Milt said.

"A tall glass of white wine is why I'm here, Roddy!" Kristen added with a smile.

"No better reason!" Roddy replied. There is a booth open at the back. Music is a little less loud there. Be right over with your drinks!"

Kristen and Milt sat down in the booth Roddy had recommended and took their jackets off. Milt glanced at Kristen, who was still looking around the room at the young crowd.

"Well, this is unusual," he said. "What have I done to deserve this date? Or am I in trouble?"

Kristen turned back to Milt. "Are these people in here even old enough to drink?"

"Kristen!" Milt said. "Stop with that shit. You never want to go out for a drink. What's going on?"

"I talked to Carol Biggs today at East End Grocers on her break. I asked her about her son Randy's death, which happened around the same time as Rick's plane crash thirteen years ago."

Milt sat straight up and moved himself to the back of the booth with a thud. "You did what!?"

"That's why I wanted to come here!" Kristen said. "I didn't want the kids to overhear any of this."

"I don't know if I want to overhear any of this. Where are our drinks!" Milt looked over at the bar.

"Milt, listen to me. She thinks Randy's death wasn't an accident."

Roddy came to the booth with their drinks. "There you go, folks! One tall glass of white wine! One cold beer! Enjoy!"

"Thanks, Roddy!" Milt said with a strained smile. As Roddy walked away, he turned back to Kristen. "That's crazy, Kristen! Why would you bring that up with her! We don't know if anything Oakey said was true!"

"What did Oakey say, Milt? Nothing! He just said Randy didn't die from falling through thin ice, but he was thinking it! He was thinking he was murdered by the DeMellos."

Milt moved forward in his seat and leaned on the table. "So that is what Carol Biggs said? The DeMellos murdered her son?"

"She didn't say who killed him, but she blames this Fritz Rine...Rinesten...whatever the fuck his name is who owned the plane! She seems to think he controls a lot in this town, including the DeMello twins and the cops!"

Milt took a drink of his beer. "Christ. This is all fucked up. Didn't you say the DeMellos were just not good people? Now they're fucking murderers! Who's overreacting now, Kristen?" He looked around to make sure no one could overhear their conversation.

"What exactly does Carol Biggs expect you to do?"

"Actually, nothing!" Kristen said, sitting back. "She doesn't think it really much matters what she does after all this time, and she is worried about her job."

"Okay, then case closed," Milt said. "Good riddance!"

"Well...maybe not," Kristen replied, taking a sip of her wine. "What about you going to the police station to see if you can get the original police report?"

"Oh no! I'm not getting mixed up in that shit!"

Kristen didn't reply. She took an even bigger sip of her wine.

"Oh, c'mon, Kristen! I've just started a new job as union rep for the workers at Rennet, and now you want me to become some fucking detective? I've had enough of the cops with Rick's gold crap!"

"Just think about it."

"This is crazy." Milt rubbed his forehead. "And now do you at least believe me why I want the boys to stay away from the DeMello kid! Changed your mind on their trip yet?"

"No, they can go," Kristen said calmly. "Like you said, the gold is long gone. If there was something the DeMellos wanted up there, they would have found it long ago. It has nothing to do with the boys." She looked over at the jukebox, which had stopped playing music. "You have a quarter? This generation doesn't know music worth shit!"

Chapter Seventeen

# OUTDOOR EDUCATION

Nathan drove into the Riley Hardware store parking lot as John reached into the truck glove compartment and pulled out their list of supplies for their long-weekend camping trip. They were now into the second week of May, and daytime temperatures had the boys finally shedding their coats for sweatshirts.

"I don't know if we have enough money for all of this," John said, looking over the list. "Why did you have to go and buy this stupid CB radio for the truck? Waste of money for our trip!"

"Hey, it was a straight trade with Brad Silgosh for my old floor speakers in the basement. With the big antenna on the back, I bet we could get ten to fifteen miles. Somebody might be in range!"

John shook his head. "Okay, let's go in. Let's see how far we can get."

The two boys walked around the hardware store, picking up their list of supplies. They bought a new Coleman lantern to replace a broken one at home, small hatchet, waterproof matches, nails, water container, and lighter fluid. They stopped at the back of the store, where they saw a three-person tent set up on display as the latest in camping gear.

"Man, that's what we need, John," Nathan said, turning to his brother.

John came over to take a closer look. He peeked inside and felt the material. "This beats Dad's tarp tent hands down! Probably fifty pounds lighter, too!"

"Hello, boys!"

Nathan and John turned to see Frank Riley, the store's owner, standing behind them, smiling.

"You know, they use this on Mount Everest!" he said, walking around the tent. "Waterproof nylon, super-light aluminum pole construction, and easy to put up! You boys in need of one, because I could probably cut you a deal on this display?"

Nathan and John looked at each other. "I could go into my savings," Nathan said to John.

"I don't think Mom and Dad would want you spending university money on a tent," John replied.

Frank interjected, "Well, let me ask what you are using it for? Where are you going?"

"We're going up to Yars Lake on the May long weekend," Nathan said. "Little trip just to explore."

"Yars Lake? That's off the Bitman logging road, right?"

"About forty miles up and then a two- to three-mile hike in," said John.

"Yeah, I was up there a few years ago." Frank walked from behind the tent and back over to the boys. "You know, I don't usually try to lose a sale, but why don't you boys just stay in that abandoned trapper's cabin up there? Still in good shape, and everyone does it!"

"The trapper's cabin? You mean the cabin of the guy who found the crashed plane?" Nathan asked.

"You got it!" Frank said. "But he died years ago...or went missing. Who knows? The guy was a hermit. He never did like all the attention the Stinson Mine plane crash brought to him."

"Berts never said anything about him going missing in the book," John whispered over to Nathan.

"Don't know," Nathan whispered back.

"You know what, Mr. Riley? That's a good idea!" Nathan said. "We'll check that cabin out when we get up there. Thanks for the tip!"

"Not a problem." A bell went off, signalling another customer had entered the store and causing Frank to look away. "Well, I have other customers, boys. Why don't you bring the rest of that stuff up to the front counter, and I'll ring you through. At least I'll make some sales today!"

Nathan and John set their items on the counter as Frank began to take the tags off and enter the numbers into the cash register. He looked over his glasses as he picked up a compass. "You know I have a metal detector at the back, boys, if you really want to make this trip professional. You wouldn't be the first people to go up there and look for the gold."

Nathan and John both smiled. "No, we are good, Mr. Riley. We really are just going up to explore and fish. If there is gold up there, we just hope to trip over it."

Frank laughed. "Alright, can't blame you. Enough people have wasted money on that wild goose chase." He bagged the supplies for the boys as Nathan placed a stack of bills on the counter.

Frank rang in the money and handed the change back to Nathan. "Well, look, at least bring me back some of that Yars Lake pickerel, alright? That's gold in itself!"

"Will do, Mr. Riley," John replied

The two boys exchanged looks as they headed out the door to the truck.

"Is that the only reason anybody goes up to Yars Lake anymore?" John asked.

"It's probably always on everyone's mind, but like Mr. Riley said, the fishing is damn good, too," Nathan replied. "Let him think what he wants."

"But what about Chad's dad and uncle? Do you think they would give a shit if they knew we are going up there?" John asked as the brothers placed their packages in the back of the truck. "Maybe Chad said something. Maybe we should do this trip some other time."

"Not after buying all this crap." Nathan lifted another heavy package over the side, and then he looked back at John across the box of the truck. "We're not changing anything. They have no idea that we are going up to Yars Lake, let alone when, so stop worrying. All Chad saw was a map we had out at school. And truth is, we have no fucking idea where the gold is, and Dad is probably right; it was picked up by Stinson Mine years ago!"

The two boys got into the truck.

"And you know as well as I do, we'll probably see Chad up there anyway on one of his survival trips," Nathan said. "He should be teaching the high school outdoor education class!"

John laughed. "Yeah, you are probably right. I think I have been reading too many mystery novels."

Nathan started the truck. "You got that right. And speaking of outdoor education, don't be bringing any of the DeMello shit up again with Dad before we go. We'll tell him we might stay in the trapper's cabin, but that's it!"

"Nope. Learned my lesson on that one. No talk of the DeMellos!" John replied.

"DeMellos!" Nathan said, laughing. "Fuck 'em. We'll be up there and back with the gold before they know what hit them!"

He put the truck in gear and exited the parking lot, with the truck's tires spitting gravel.

## Chapter Eighteen

# ALL IN

"Hey, Franky, how are ya?" David said as he stepped into the back room of the hardware store. He and Marty sat down at an eight-foot round wooden table with six chairs placed around the outside.

"I'm good, Davey. You boys ready to lose all your hard-earned money to support my store expansion tonight?"

"You're fucking dreaming, Riley," David said as he checked out the wobbly table. "Why don't you start by fixing this fucking table."

"It will fix itself when all the money comes to my side!" Frank said with a smile. He turned his head to a knock at the back of the room.

He opened the back door, and two other men stepped in. He shook hands with each. "Glad you could make it, boys. Have a seat. I'll get us some drinks, and we'll get started."

Dom Santtini and Craig Strobass shook hands with Marty and David and sat down.

Frank Riley had been hosting his six friends from high school for a poker game twice a year for the past twenty years. He called their poker group "the last of the Tear Falls Mohicans" for having stayed in the small town and, as he termed it, "toughed it out." He knew they had drifted their separate ways on many things, but nobody asked too many questions about anyone's personal business. Nobody cared. Everyone had their own shit to contend with in life. Poker was a time to win a few bucks, drink, and say anything that wouldn't go beyond the rooms' four walls.

"Where's Johnny?" David asked, pulling back the empty chair beside him.

"He's taking a pass. His wife didn't take kindly to him losing their trip money the last time he was here and being pulled over by the cops on the way home," Craig Strobass said.

"Shit, I told that fucking guy to take the ice road. They can't ticket you on a road that is only there six months of the year," David replied.

"He did. Or at least, he tried to. Got to the boat ramp, and Singh was waiting for him. Ticketed him before he drove down onto the ice."

"Fuck, I miss McIntyre," Marty said as he grabbed the deck of cards and began shuffling. "At least that guy would just ask you to give him your bottle of booze instead of ticketing you for it." He laughed.

Santtini leaned over the table. "Singh is into more than just tickets. He's been poking his head around Rennet a lot lately, too."

David looked over at Santtini and gave him a long, blank stare. Marty understood his brother's non-verbal and quickly cut the deck of cards.

"How fucked up is that, eh, boys?" Marty said as he hurriedly dealt the cards. "Used to be the brown guy took the bribes and the white man was the good guy. Only Tear Falls could fuck that up."

David picked up his cards while still staring at Santtini. "What'd you mean he's been poking around Rennet? Poking around for what?"

"Saw him in Danny Henry's union office a few weeks ago. Figure the cops don't pay courtesy visits to Rennet unless something is up," Santtini replied.

Marty looked over at Santtini as he placed the deck of cards aside. "Hey, Dom, why don't you shut the fuck up and play. We're not here to make any hero stories out of Singh."

David threw a twenty-dollar bill in the centre of the table and looked back at his cards. "Yup, a cop actually doing his fucking job. Who would have guessed?"

The men spent the next four hours playing cards, drinking, and telling old high school stories, but Marty could tell his brother wasn't focused. He kept folding good hands and betting on lousy ones. He was glad to finally see Santtini and Strobass rise up from their chairs and say they had to leave.

Frank Riley walked them to the door, putting a hand on each of their shoulders. "Don't try and take any ice roads home tonight, alright, boys? Don't want to have a drunk water rescue on my hands."

The two men laughed as they left out the back door. Frank came back to the table and looked at the stack of money in front of Marty. "Care to share, you lucky bastard?"

"It's all skill, Franky," Marty replied, grinning.

Frank collected the empty beer bottles as David watched his brother count his money. "Guess no expansion money tonight, eh, Franky?" David said with a laugh.

Frank brought the bottles over to an empty beer case on the counter by the fridge and started placing them in. "I'll survive, Davey," he said over his shoulder. "Besides, things are picking up with the spring camping and fishing season starting. Had a few high school kids, the Tonkin boys, come in the other day and clean me out for a trip up to Yars Lake."

David leaned his chair back on its two hind legs as he exchanged glances with his brother. "Yars Lake. The Tonkin kids."

Frank returned to the table with three shot glasses and a bottle of Southern Comfort. He sat down and poured shots as he said, "Yup, and don't ask me where that younger generation gets the money. But what the fuck do I care as long as it's going into my till."

David leaned his chair back down and crossed his arms in front of him. "They say when they are going, Frank? What day?"

Frank sat back and rotated his shot glass on the table. "Why, you scared they are going to beat you to some big fish up there, Dave? Or maybe…" He leaned over the table with his arms crossed. "…to some big fucking pot of gold at the end of a rainbow," he finished with a smirk.

David looked back at Frank and smiled. He threw the table up, knocking Frank back out of his chair and onto his back. The Southern Comfort smashed to the floor, and his brother's money scattered across the room. He approached Frank and grabbed him by the neck as Frank tried to get up. He held a closed fist above his head. "You know, Frank, it's a good thing we go way back. Otherwise, you would be the one having a little accident with the lake this time of year."

"Take it easy, Dave," Frank said, putting up his hands to shield his face. "They said the May long weekend. Fuck, I was going to tell you."

Marty walked over and stood over the two men. "He was going to tell us, Dave. Frank tends to do stupid things when he's drunk." He squatted down. "Right, Frank?"

"Yeah…yeah," Frank said, looking up at David with fearful eyes. "Just had too much to drink. That's all."

David stood up, and Marty helped Frank to his feet.

Frank walked over to the fridge and leaned his back against the counter, breathing heavily. David picked up the table as Marty went around the room and collected his money.

"Thanks for the hospitality, Frank. I think we'll head out now," David said. He looked at Frank's broken chair on the floor. "Sorry about the chair, but I guess you have the tools to fix it."

"Yeah, don't worry about it," Frank said, staring at the chair and trying to catch his breath. He looked up. "You guys drive safe…okay?"

"We will. And you never know, Frank. If we get stopped by Singh, maybe your expansion money will come in handy!"

## Chapter Nineteen

# GALVERSON

M arty and David DeMello pulled up outside the Country Baron Tavern at 6 p.m. and parked their pickup truck. They got out and dusted the sawdust off from a day's work at their sawmill. They opened the front door and approached a small, dimly lit counter, where a waitress was sorting bills.

"Can I help you gentlemen?" she asked.

"We're here to meet someone," David said.

"Name?" She looked at the two men with obvious disapproval.

"Fritz. Fritz Rinestein."

Marty hit David on the shoulder. "There he is. Over in the back corner."

"We see him," David said to the waitress. "We'll show ourselves back."

The waitress went to hand the two men menus, but David brushed her off. "Drinks are all we need."

The Country Baron was the only restaurant in town to attempt to offer anything resembling fine dining. The restaurant provided wood-grained armchairs for seating and tables with white table linens. Cutlery was arranged on cloth napkins, and place settings contained a set of wine glasses to accompany thick, polygon-shaped drinking glasses. The restaurant was lit by overhanging, circular stained-glass lights, and a paisley rug lined the floor to dampen the noise of footsteps. One set of booths lined the back of the restaurant and was usually reserved for its best customers.

Marty and David sat down in Fritz's booth and stayed silent as they watched him consume his steak and read a newspaper beside him.

He spoke without looking up. "You shitheads want to tell me why you come in here and the first thing you do is embarrass me?"

"Sorry, Fritz," said Marty. "We just got off work and thought you would want to hear the news as soon as possible. We won't be staying long."

Fritz looked up at the twins. "Nahh…that part, you got wrong. Now you are going to stay all fucking night, because everybody in this restaurant knows you're here to wash the dishes…right? Not to be meeting with a respected pilot in his flight uniform. Let me call someone over to take you to the kitchen!" Fritz put his arm up to call the waitress over.

Marty and David had met Fritz Rinestein for the first time fifteen years ago when Fritz had agreed to sponsor their hockey team as a part of his ongoing attempt to build his reputation in the community. They knew Fritz to be a calculated and precise businessman. He despised anything or anyone that might tarnish his standing as a successful, caring member of Tear Falls. He believed his image was at the heart of his success in the drug trade, and he was ruthless in its defense.

David jumped up to intercept the waitress as she approached the booth. He pulled out a hundred-dollar bill and whispered in her ear. She took the hundred dollars, nodded, and left.

Fritz looked at David as he sat down. "Better be good for having to put up with your shit!" he said. He took a sip of his wine. "Before you two start flapping your mouths about something stupid, what happened with the Queensway truck at the border?"

"That was Beenie Marson driving that truck, Fritz. One of the empty containers was rolling around in the cab. The stupid bastard tried to say he had it because he was a part-time scientist."

Fritz stuck his fork into his mashed potatoes. "Beenie, that crazy fuck. And I suppose the cops took everything?"

"Everything including the container. Questioned Beenie for a long time," David said.

"Yeah, well, let's see if our part-time scientist knew enough to keep his fucking mouth shut."

Fritz put his knife and fork down and wiped his mouth with his napkin. "Okay, make it quick. I fly out at nine. What is the big news that I am going to be so glad to hear from you two slobs?"

"We have some new information on the lost gold," David said.

"Oh fuck, this should be good," Fritz said, sitting back. He took a drink of his wine. "Go ahead, I'm listening."

"Marty's kid, Chad, knows the two high school boys of Torrison's best friend, Milt Tonkin," David said. "They are arranging a trip up to Yars Lake for the May long weekend to do a search. Chad is convinced they know something more about the whereabouts of the gold."

"Two high school kids planning a fucking field trip," Fritz said. "That's the best you can do? Fuck, this is a waste of my time!"

Marty cut in. "Telling you, Fritz. My son said they had out a map at school. They were doing calculations. They even had the book that guy wrote about the crash. He thinks they have found out something after all these years. Maybe their dad gave them a tip. Maybe their dad said something in his sleep. Who the fuck knows?"

"Oh, right, the book," Fritz said. "That bastard has been trying to put Tear Falls on the map now for years. Nobody believes his bullshit. Nothing that would help anyone find the gold, anyways."

The waitress interrupted the men's conversation by returning to the booth and uncorking a bottle of red wine. She set two more glasses in front of the twins and placed the bottle on the table with the label facing Fritz. He picked it up. "Ah...Caymus!" he said. "You guys have great fucking taste in wine, but not clothes. Now that's fucked up!"

Fritz filled all three wine glasses. "This Tonkin guy, he was a friend of Torrison's, right? Worked with him? And didn't they question him after the crash?"

"McIntyre brought him in. Even the RCMP spoke with Tonkin. But he denied knowing shit," David replied. "But McIntyre told us Galverson paid Tonkin a visit to give him some of Torrison's guns, which he thinks Galverson took from the plane after the crash. They could have talked."

"Yeah, there must be something they know, Fritz. Something doesn't make sense," Marty said.

"It doesn't make sense," Fritz repeated. "You fucking don't make sense!" Trying to control his rising voice, he took a large drink of his wine and leaned over the table, giving a hard stare to both men. "You boys know what's happening here, right? You're fucking smart enough to figure it out? Ever since you let my plane get stolen by that asshole Torrison, I've had to pay."

"Biggs was an asshole for letting that happen," David said.

Fritz turned to David, pointing a finger. "No, you're an asshole for letting it happen. You got Biggs that fucking job, and he fucked up. Now I'm even getting fucked at the border and can't pay my bills because my name doesn't mean shit anymore. I need my name back like the old days so people in this town know it's worth working with me. You fucking understand? You understand how this all fucking works?"

"We understand, Fritz," Marty said.

"You fuckheads better, because if I can't pay my bills soon, I'm going to be looking for someone to pay them for me." Fritz pushed his finished dinner plate forward and threw his napkin on the table.

"Alright! I don't see shit in any of this that says these kids know where the gold is, but you find out. You follow these little fucks up there and find out whether their dad had some sort of fucked-up revelation that he needed to say something." Fritz motioned to the waitress again and made a gesture with his hands for her to bring the bill.

"We're going to find it, Fritz," David said. "It's going to look good on you. We're going to get your reputation back. We promise!"

Fritz stood up and put on his flight suit jacket. "Yeah. Like the way you found Galverson?" he said. "Where the fuck did he disappear to? You guys couldn't even find a fucking old man in his cabin, and you expect me to believe you can find my gold?"

"He just up and disappeared, Fritz! He was fucked in the head to start with!" Marty said.

David smacked Marty on the side of the head. He looked back up at Fritz. "We'll find the gold, Fritz. Don't worry about that. And we'll call you as soon as we do."

The waitress came over and handed Fritz the bill. He threw it on the table and straightened his tie. "Yeah, you do that. Call me. In the meantime, pay that bill and leave the young lady a good tip. And do yourselves a fuckin' favour and go out the back door!"

Chapter Twenty

# CAMPBELL CABIN

Milt sat in Danny Henry's union office, staring at a spiral-bound book. He flexed it back and forth in his hand to judge the weight and then threw it on the steel desk and put his head back.

Danny Henry walked in. "You don't have a headache already, do you, Milt?" he said with a smile.

"Not a chance... Just stretching, Danny." Milt straightened up as Danny went behind his desk and sat down. Danny picked up the spiral-bound book on the union's collective agreement with the mine and handed it back to Milt. "I know it's as dry as shit, Milt, but you're going to have to know this as well as the Bible, or in your case at least, your hunting guide."

"No, I've read it, Danny. You don't mind if I call you on a few things, though, after you retire next month?"

"No, you can do that. But you are going to have to think on the fly in meetings with management. They can get pretty tough, and there is nothing they like more than a weak union rep!"

Milt put on his glasses and started flipping through the pages. "This is what you used to fight for Rick and Oakey? It's all in here?"

"Pretty much," Danny said. He reached into his desk drawer, took out a brown file folder with a name on it, and placed it on his desk. "Let me ask you something before I give you your first file, Milt. Did you take this job because of what happened to Rick and Oakey?"

"I guess I saw them as an example of how workers can be treated badly. So…yeah, maybe," Milt said. "Why?"

"Because it has to go beyond that, Milt. You're going to have to represent the workers you don't like. Maybe even hate." Danny handed Milt the brown file folder.

Milt looked up at the top and saw the name written in black marker.

He looked back at Danny. "Oh, c'mon, Danny. You got to be kidding me. This is my first file? Trent Campbell. This fucker… this guy is more trouble for other workers than he is for the mine. Rick hated him!"

"Yup. I know," Danny said. "That's why I asked you the question." He handed Milt a paper outlining Campbell's recent suspension report from Rennet Mine.

Milt read over the brief details and looked back at Danny.

"Stealing? Air tights from the Rennet Mine lab. What the fuck are air tights?"

"Don't know exactly," Danny replied. "They told me it's a glass sealed container so nothing gets in or out. Pretty expensive shit as I understand it. Apparently, they have been going missing for the past year. Everyone just thought it was the guy on the previous shift who broke one or they were being misplaced."

"Isn't Campbell close to retirement? Why would he take the chance to steal?"

"Your guess is as good as mine, Milt. But workers getting close to retirement get worried. Maybe Campbell is selling jars of pickles on the side. I don't know. But like it or not, you'll have to talk to him at some point."

"Shit, you had to do it to me, didn't you," Milt said as he put the paper into the file.

"Like I said, Milt, you can't pick and choose in this job," Danny replied. "It's not about you, what makes you uncomfortable. It's about doing what's right." Danny leaned back and tapped his pen on the desk. "You can do that, right, Milt? Fight for the underdog? Even if that person means nothing to you?"

Milt could sense some doubt from Danny. "Yeah…of course!" he said. "I will take the file home and read it right away."

"Good!" Danny said. "Let's meet back here in two weeks. Give you lots of time to read more of the collective agreement and go out and see Campbell. Management meeting is in three."

Milt drove his pickup truck down Highway 205, keeping his eyes peeled for the turnoff to Trent Campbell's cabin road. He was already ten miles on the other side of Tear Falls and wondering how the hell Campbell even made it to work on time, let alone put in a full shift. He spotted a small green sign with the words "Bull-Rush Road." He put his blinker on, turned, and drove two miles down a dirt road pitted with potholes.

He stopped the truck as he came to a sign tacked to a tree with an arrow pointing down a one-car-wide bush lane. "Campbell Cabin—This Way!" Milt read aloud.

He drove another five hundred feet and came into a large clearing. He parked his truck and gazed through his windshield at Trent Campbell's cabin. The yard was strewn with car parts and household debris and was overgrown with tall grass. He examined the weathered and torn wood siding and let out a sigh. "Why can't this asshole just live off the land and retire now," he said. He picked up his zippered leather carrying case and went to knock on the door.

"Hello," he said as a woman answered. "I was looking for Trent, Trent Campbell?"

"He's out right now, but he should be back soon. Is there something I can help you with?"

Milt looked at the heavyset woman dressed in jeans and an untucked mustard-coloured dress shirt. Her dirty blonde hair was pulled back in a ponytail. She had no makeup on, and the visible lines on her face had Milt estimating she was in her late fifties.

"I'm Milt Tonkin," he said, unsure of how much he should divulge. "I'm his union rep from Rennet. I was supposed to meet him here at ten?"

"Oh, yes. Hi, come in. I'm his wife, Lisa," she said as she opened the door for him. "Have a seat. Would you like a coffee while you wait?"

"Sure. One cream, one sugar, please."

Lisa left as Milt looked around the large main room. It held a collection of mixed furniture, table lamps, and odd knickknacks placed on every available surface. Coiled-rope rugs lay on the rough wooden floor in front of each sitting area, and an aged, peeling coffee table ran the length of a worn sofa. Numerous hand-painted pictures of wildlife adorned the walls, and there was a large framed photograph above the wood fireplace. Milt recognized it right away. He stood up and walked over to study the aerial photograph of Rennet Mine.

"That was given to Trent by a friend of his, Pat Galverson, who was a pilot," Lisa said as she re-entered the room with a tray and two coffees. She placed the tray on the coffee table and sat down.

Milt turned around abruptly. "Pat...? Pat Galverson of Brown Airways?"

"Yeah, did you know him?" Lisa asked.

Milt sat down, still concentrating on the photograph. "Friend of mine did. Long time ago."

He turned his attention back to his work and unzipped his carrying case. "Do you think Trent is going to be long?"

"I don't think so. He is dropping off our son at my mother's and running a few errands. I'm sure he is anxious to meet with you. He still doesn't know why he was suspended from Rennet for just a few late shifts."

Milt stopped with his paperwork. "Late shifts...?" he said, looking at Lisa.

"Yeah, Trent says they can be pretty picky at Rennet. Well, you would know, being the union rep."

"Yeah, for sure. They are picky for being late. I'll make sure we talk about that."

"So, you think you can get him back to work, Mr. Tonkin?" Lisa asked, taking a sip of her coffee. "Rennet has been real good to us, you know."

Milt could feel the distress in Lisa's voice. No matter what he thought of Trent Campbell, he realized a family was depending on his income.

"I'll certainly try, Mrs. Campbell," he said with a forced smile. "Every family needs money coming in."

"Oh, it's more than the money, Mr. Tonkin. It's everything they have done for our disabled son."

Milt paused. He placed his pen down on his paperwork and sat back on the sofa. "You have a disabled son, Mrs. Campbell?"

"Yes, he has cerebral palsy. He has to use a power wheelchair to get around. Well, it's broken down right now, so Trent has been trying to get him a new one. There is nothing Trent wouldn't do for him, and Rennet has helped a lot. Want to see what Trent has made for him?"

"Yeah…sure," Milt said, feeling he didn't have much of a choice. Lisa stood up, and Milt followed. She led him to a room and opened the door. "This is our son Dylan's bedroom."

Milt's eyebrows instinctively raised as he scanned the room. In the corner was a large walk-in shower. The tiling was the same colour found in the Rennet washrooms, and he recognized the tubing running out of a false back for water as that used for the mine hoses. He looked over the bed to see metal tracks in the ceiling. A small winch with a sling attached hung from one of the tracks. The winch was etched with the mine logo, and the sling had the words "Property of Rennet Mine" painted on it in red.

Lisa leaned slightly forward and stared at Milt's face. "You're impressed, I see! She looked back at the room and waved her hand across her body in a showroom gesture. "All of this, Mr. Tonkin, is what the Rennet Mine has given Trent to help our son. Trent couldn't have done it without them!"

Milt looked back at Lisa. Over her shoulder, he noticed a portable folding metal ramp from Rennet in the corner of the room. "This...this was all donated by Rennet?" he asked, trying to hide his astonishment.

"Yes. Now, Trent had to put in the work, of course. He has more things out in the shed, but that stuff didn't work out." She walked back out of the room, and Milt followed.

He rubbed his hand through his hair as he sat down on the sofa. *What the hell did Danny get me into?* he thought. He looked up. "Mrs. Campbell, how much does Rennet and the government help with your son's care?"

"They try, but it always comes up short. They helped with Dylan's first wheelchair, but they won't help with a new one. And anything extra is all on us. I mean, what's the use of having a wheelchair if you can't get it in and out of the cabin with a ramp, right?" She took a moment to hand Milt his coffee. "And the van to carry Dylan's wheelchair, well, that cost Trent his boat to get that."

Milt placed his coffee down. He sat up and clasped his hands together, interlocking his fingers as he touched his mouth.

"And if Trent doesn't get his job back, what then? What would you do?"

He watched as Lisa turned her gaze to the floor. "I...I don't know, Mr. Tonkin. Dylan's new wheelchair is only half paid for. It's sitting at the Becker Pharmacy in town right now, and they said they can't budge on the price." She looked back up with tear-flushed eyes. "Trent said maybe the town would give him a job. Or maybe even the DeMello sawmill. He's been trying to stop by there when he can to see if they have anything."

Milt took a deep breath. He could feel his heart start to pound.

"Mrs. Campbell, I think I better reschedule my meeting with your husband. I have to get back to town, and I don't want to rush this with him. I think I will talk to Danny Henry, the other union rep at Rennet. He is retiring soon, but I'm sure he will help me out with Trent's grievance."

"Thank you, Mr. Tonkin. Thank you so much. I guess you see this is as a little bit more than Trent just losing his job."

"Oh, I can see that, Mrs. Campbell," Milt replied as he hastily put his paperwork back in his case and zipped it up. He stood up and walked to the door. He turned and shook Lisa Campbell's hand as he stared around the cabin. "Is that a hospital bed I see there over by the window?"

"Yes," Lisa said, turning and looking in the same direction. She turned back and smiled. "We put that there so Dylan can watch the stars over the river at night. It cost over—"

"Two thousand dollars," Milt said.

"Yeah, how did you know that, Mr. Tonkin?"

"Lucky guess," he replied as he turned to open the door. "I will be in touch, Mrs. Campbell."

"Thank you again, Mr. Tonkin!" she replied as she watched Milt head for his truck.

Milt got into his truck and took a moment to put his head down on the steering wheel. He was already emotionally exhausted, and he hadn't even asked Trent Campbell one question. He was starting to wonder if this whole mess was some sort of test by Danny to see if he was right for the job. He lifted his head and stared at the cabin. Then he reached down and started the truck. If it was, he was going to pass with flying colours!

## Chapter Twenty-One

# TALK AND SINGH

"You know, it might be a little early to be trying to get a tan in the middle of May there, Mr. Sunshine," Kristen said, standing on the back porch. She walked down the porch steps and approached Milt, who was sitting in a plaid green webbed aluminum lawn chair. He was stretched out, wearing shorts, unlaced work boots, and a light blue windbreaker over a t-shirt. Sunglasses shaded his eyes, and a beer bottle rested in his hands. His son John's portable tape player was belting out a Burton Cummings song, "Fine State of Affairs."

"Milt, are you okay?" Kristen asked, standing in front of him with her hands on her hips. "You want me to join you in my bikini?" She gave him a nudge with her foot. "Hey…are you even listening to me? How did your meeting with Trent Campbell go this morning?"

Milt took off his sunglasses and sat up. He turned off the music and looked up at Kristen. "I'm not sure if I'm cut out for this union rep job. I'm no Danny Henry."

"It went that well, did it," Kristen replied. "Let me get another chair." She walked behind Milt to their shed, opened the door, and took out another lawn chair. She walked back, unfolded it, placed it at right angles to Milt, and sat down. "Nobody is a Danny Henry, Milt. Now, give me a beer and tell me what happened."

Milt obeyed, handing Kristen a beer from a small cooler.

"I don't know, hon. I always have all these good intentions in my head, and then I get sideswiped, I get in over my head. And to be honest, this morning, I was fucking drowning."

"Well, that tells me a lot. All of this from just trying to help Trent Campbell? A person who everyone thinks is a jerk!"

Milt looked down at the grass while swinging his beer bottle between his hands. "He is a jerk, Kristen. But now I'm wondering if it's for all the right reasons." He shifted his gaze to her. "He is stealing from Rennet, alright. Probably been doing it for years. But he has been doing it to support his disabled son."

Kristen sat back in her chair and crossed her legs. She took a deep breath and stared off into the distance. "I thought they placed their son in a special home out of town years ago."

"Apparently not. And he needs one of those electric wheelchairs, which I imagine doesn't come cheap. Trent wasn't even home when I got there. His wife was practically in tears about it."

Kristen looked back at Milt. "Milt, you can't be doing this. You're a union rep. You're not a social worker, and you're not children's aid. You can't solve everyone's problems or take responsibility for them. It's too much for you."

"Is it? You know where Trent Campbell was when I asked his wife? She said he was stopping by the DeMello sawmill to look for work."

Kristen took a long drink of her beer. She brushed the curls of her brown hair back. "Why is it the DeMellos seem to be at the centre of everybody's shit in this town, Milt? If it's not Carol Biggs for me, it's Trent Campbell for you." She placed her beer beside her chair and placed her head back, her eyes closed to feel the sun. "And it seems there is nothing anybody can fucking do about it."

Kristen felt a beer being placed in her lap. "Here, drink this one, too," Milt said.

She opened her eyes to see him walking to the porch. "Where are you going?"

"I can't do anything about all the shit the DeMello's have caused, Kristen, but maybe I can get someone to start cleaning it up!"

Minutes later, he was running from his parked truck and opening the door of the Ontario Provincial Police station for Tear Falls. He stepped into an empty waiting room and looked at his watch, which showed 5:30 p.m. He wondered if he were too late. A young police officer stepped out of a side office and looked at him.

"Can I help you, sir?"

"Oh...hello. Just wanted to ask a question about reports. How do I get a police report?" Milt said.

"What, like a car accident report? You want to report an accident?" the officer asked.

"No, I was more interested in an old report the police would have filed on an accident."

The officer walked around behind the counter, opposite Milt.

"You would have to come back when administration is in. They leave at three on weekends. Just me and the sergeant here right now." The officer pointed over to a lighted office. "When did the accident happen? Maybe it was even me that filed it."

"I doubt it. January 1972."

"Oh shit! I wasn't even on the force yet!" Then, glancing over Milt's shoulder, the officer said, "Oh, hi, sir!"

Milt turned to see an older officer walking toward him. He could clearly see the stripes of a sergeant on his sleeve. "There a problem here, Marsh?"

"No problem, sir. This man was just asking about how to get a police report from 1972."

"Nineteen seventy-two?" the sergeant said. He looked at Milt and back to Marsh. "Shouldn't you be out on patrol? I can deal with this."

"Right, sir!"

The Sergeant turned back to Milt. "I'm Sergeant Singh. We don't get many requests for reports from that long ago. What's this all about?"

"Well, I don't know how long you have been here, Sergeant…"

"Four years!"

"Yeah…well, okay, I'm looking for information on an accident that happened to the son of Carol…of a friend of ours. An ice fishing accident. He drowned on Fenny Lake in January of 1972."

"A drowning. All the way back to 1972," Singh said. "Come back to my office. We can talk there. I need to listen for the phone and radio that's in my office."

Milt followed the sergeant into his office and took a seat. He looked around the room and could see a number of hanging awards and family pictures showing Sergeant Singh's Asian ethnicity.

"So, let's start off by me getting your name," Singh said.

"Milt Tonkin." Milt reached out and to shake Singh's hand, but the sergeant declined to look up as he continued to make notes.

"Okay, Mr. Tonkin. You can file a request for any information that you want during normal business hours. Can't tell you what we'll find after all these years, but we'll look." The sergeant's head turned to the radio as some voices came on.

"But they don't destroy those reports, right?" Milt asked. "Reports when someone dies or is killed, do they?"

Singh turned back to Milt. "I thought you said this was an accident. A drowning."

"Well, yeah, it was a drowning, but same thing, right? I mean, someone has died, so they would keep the report?"

Singh crossed his arms and looked at Milt. "Look, Mr. Tonkin. I'm a busy man. When I took over this detachment four years ago, half the files were incomplete or missing. So, I don't hold out much hope, but why don't you at least give me a name, and I will do a search myself. Leave me your number, and if I come up with anything, I will call you."

"Okay, that's fair. That would be a big help," Milt said.

Singh handed Milt a pen and paper, and he wrote down the information and handed it back.

"You probably recognize the last name of Biggs. I think a lot of people from around here at least know the family," Milt said.

Singh looked up at Milt. "Do I look like I'm from around here, Mr. Tonkin?" He put the paper in his desk drawer and got up from his chair. "I will show you out. We close the detachment doors to the public at six."

"Sure, I understand," Milt said. "Hey, thanks for taking the information!"

"You're welcome," Singh said, showing Milt the door.

Milt arrived home and came through the front door. "Kristen!" he yelled.

Kristen came around the corner. "What is it, Milt! You're late for dinner!"

"Want to go to the NearNorth for a drink after dinner?" he said, smiling as he brushed by her to sit at the kitchen table.

"Yeah...I guess... What?"

Chapter Twenty-Two

# DRIP CASTLE

"O kay, boys, I know you said you are going to stay in the old trapper's cabin this weekend, but I'm going to put the tent in the truck anyway. It's in my hockey bag here if you need it. Poles and pegs are in there, too."

"Thanks, Dad!" Nathan said.

John loaded their two backpacks in the truck as Nathan crossed the items off the list. "How can we have this much stuff for three days of camping?" Nathan said.

"I don't know," John said as he opened the truck passenger door and placed a portable tape player on the floor and a bag of cassettes in the glove compartment.

"Oh no! You are not bringing that boombox on a camping trip!"

"Why not? We need some tunes at night. And it has a radio so we can keep track of the weather."

"Alright. But you're carrying it!"

Kristen came out of the house. "Well, at least you two lucked out on a nice, sunny spring day today. Heard it's going to rain the rest of the weekend. You packed your raincoats?"

"Yes, Mom," Nathan said. "We can always come home if it gets too bad. We're just an hour or so away up Bitman road."

"Okay. Don't fault your mom for worrying."

"I think we are good, John," Nathan said. "Let's get going. It's eight now. We can be at Yars Lake by ten if we leave now."

"Hold up!" Milt said as he brought out a soft-covered gun carrying pouch. "Here, Nathan. Take this. It's your Uncle Rick's twelve-gauge. Oakey has Rick's rifle, so it's only fair you have his other gun."

"Thanks, Dad. We'll shoot some partridge if we run out of food!"

"Never mind any of that!" Kristen said. "You two boys come home if you get hungry."

"We will, Mom," John said.

The two boys jumped in the truck. "First, some music," Nathan said as he pushed a tape into the truck's player. April Wine's "Enough Is Enough" filled the cab as Nathan backed the truck out of the driveway. They waved goodbye to their parents and headed for Yars Lake.

Kristen turned to Milt. "All is good?"

"All is good," Milt said, putting an arm around her.

After a short drive on the main highway, Nathan turned off onto the Bitman logging road. The road was made of gravel, and all vehicles that travelled down its path did so with the drone of stones being crushed and a trail of dust.

John took out their map. "I would say another three-quarters of an hour and we'll reach the cut off to Yars Lake," he said, looking over at Nathan.

"That's not bad," Nathan replied. "Any idea where that cabin might be?"

"Not on here, but it looks like there is an old mine not far from the lake. Might be worth exploring. Even if we don't find any gold, maybe we can at least say we visited an old mine!"

"That's what we'll tell mom and dad. It was a history trip!" Nathan said with a laugh.

"For sure," John replied. He opened the glove compartment and took out a tape. "Now it's my turn. Time to relax with some of my easy listening." He placed a tape into the truck's cassette player and smiled at Nathan.

"Oh no. None of your sappy karaoke shit in this truck!" Nathan replied.

"Too late!" John said as the Trooper song "Two for the Show" took over the truck's speakers.

"Should have known there would be payback," Nathan said, smiling.

Nathan yawned and looked at the truck digital clock displaying 8:57am. He knew they were close to the main trail to Yars Lake when he spotted a break in the bordering brush of the logging road.

He drove off onto a patch of well-worn ground and shut off the truck. He turned to John. "Wake up, rock star! Time to march!"

John woke up and stared out the front windshield. A dense forest stared back. "Man, that was quick. What time is it?"

"Just before nine. But we are doing okay," Nathan said.

The two brothers got out of the truck and stretched. Nathan reached into his pocket, took out a small plastic bottle of DEET, and started rubbing it on his arms and neck. He threw the bottle over to John across the front of the truck. "Put it on, or we are going to get eaten alive in that bush."

John applied the DEET and placed it in his pocket. The boys walked to the back of the truck, took out their backpacks, and harnessed them on their shoulders and waists.

"Ah, this isn't so bad," John said, flexing his legs to feel the weight of his pack on his body.

"Yeah!" Nathan said. "Give it a half-hour and then talk to me!"

Nathan took out the carry case with the shotgun and stopped and stared at the back of the truck.

"What?" John asked.

"The tent," Nathan said. "Should we take it? It's going to be a bitch to carry."

"No way. We have more important things to carry!" John reached in the truck passenger door, grabbed his boombox, and handed it to Nathan. "Here, secure this to those straps at the back of my pack."

"Man, hope this thing is worth it," Nathan said.

The brothers locked up the truck, and each placed a Boston Bruins cap on their head. They tightened the straps on their backpacks and headed to an opening in the forest marked by the faint imprint of overgrown tire tracks and a tree log spray painted with the words "Yars Lake" and an arrow pointing in the direction of the bush.

The Yars Lake trail consisted of close to three miles of thick Northern Ontario bush. There was no direct path to the lake, and beyond the initial markings, hikers were left on their own to figure out the best route. Spruce trees towered overhead, swaying occasionally, allowing rays of sunshine to reach the smaller growth below. The forest was damp in the spring and provided a competing sweet smell of new growth pine needles with rotting forest floor debris. Mosquitoes were a constant presence, but with enough repellent, their radar was sufficiently confused to make them more of annoyance than a risk for a bite.

Nathan took the lead. "You better hope that we find that cabin," he said over his shoulder. "Or you are hiking back to get the tent!"

"Told you we should have brought Chad," John said, laughing. "He would have built us a cabin on the spot."

The boys soon split up on either side of the path, walking side by side, a hundred feet apart, through the bush. It was their version of a search grid on their way to the lake. After twenty minutes of hiking, they came to a large clearing.

Nathan signalled to John to come his way. "This is not what I predicted," he said as John joined him. "This bush is way thicker than I thought. Could we have not just brought a map that says 'X marks the spot'?"

"Ah, who cares," John said. "As we told Mr. Riley, we may just get lucky and trip over a gold bar. You have to think the boxes would be spread out if they fell out of the plane. That would cover a fair amount of ground."

"Is that you or Dad talking?" Nathan replied. He took out his aluminum water bottle and unscrewed the cap. He tilted his head back to take a drink and noticed the top portion of a weathered mining head frame rising above the trees in the distance. "Is that the old mine you were talking about?"

John took out the map. "Yup, I have it circled here on the map. That's the Davidson Mine. And…" John stretched out his arm and angled his hand to the right. "We should hit Yars Lake that away. Looks like it's about half a mile."

"Okay," Nathan replied. "Let's veer our search grid in that direction. Good as any…right?"

"Now who sounds like Dad!" John said as they headed their hike northeast.

John reached the top of a small embankment and stopped walking. He looked over at Nathan and hollered, "Hey! Down there! There's the lake!"

Nathan looked back at John and pointed up to the sky, which was starting to cloud over. "Let's go!"

John reached a small strip of sand on the shoreline of Yars Lake and took off his pack. He walked toward the water's edge and squatted down. He placed his hands in the lake and could feel the cold chill as gentle ripples of water washed over his outstretched fingers. He smiled and scooped up a handful of wet sand, and then he turned and let the sand drip through his closed fingers, watching in a trance as the drops of sand fell upon one another and formed a random shape beneath.

Nathan came up from behind and watched.

"I always loved it when Dad did that with us as kids," Nathan said. He squatted down beside John and started making his own drip castle.

"No drip castle is the same," John said, imitating his dad's voice. "Every castle, like every person, is unique!"

"Like you and me," Nathan said with a smile. "Dad could make even drips of sand look good!"

"Dad can find good in anything," John replied. He grabbed another handful of sand. "But I guess maybe not the DeMellos. Why do you think Dad hates them so much?"

"I don't think he hates them," Nathan said. "But he does dislike what they stand for. It's the same reason he calls that Chris Berts an asshole. Both of them are trying to take advantage of Uncle Rick's death for their own gain."

"Yeah…maybe." John started to dig a moat around his drip castle. He stopped and stared at a handful of wet sand resting in his palm. "But sometimes I think it's more than that." He turned and looked at Nathan. "Sometimes I think it's because he has a hard time finding any good in what Uncle Rick did. I mean, he stole a plane…right? He broke the law."

Nathan stood up and admired the random architecture of his own drip castle. "I actually think it's the opposite. I think he sees everything good in what Uncle Rick did." He looked at John. "He was trying to work two jobs. He was trying to help his dying mom, and all anyone talks about is Uncle Rick stealing the gold. Maybe that's why Dad let us come up here. He likes to see us spend time together. And that's why he loved Uncle Rick. Uncle Rick was all about family. Dad will never forget that."

John rose to his feet, still holding the handful of sand. He threw it out into the lake and watched it spatter across the water, forming a cascade of small rings. "Fucking gold! Maybe we should just hide it again if we do find it!"

"Might not be a bad idea."

The boys turned their attention to a roll of thunder from the horizon.

"We better go. We need to find that cabin," Nathan said.

John stood up, went to his pack, and took out a pair of binoculars. He surveyed the shoreline of the lake before pointing to a spot for Nathan to look. "There! About halfway around the lake. Think I see a clearing and a cabin roof!"

"Good enough for me!" Nathan said. "We may have no choice!"

John picked up his pack and followed Nathan as he two-stepped over a piece of driftwood, and they began their hike down the narrow strip of beach, toward the clearing.

The beach soon gave way to a large outcropping of rock, forcing the boys to climb up and to the top of a large oval rock face.

They stopped to rest and gauge their distance from the cabin.

"Not far," Nathan said. "I would say fifteen minutes, tops."

"Looking at these clouds, I think that's all we got," John said.

The two boys took a small jump off the rock and forced their way through thick bush in an effort to hike a direct route to the cabin.

John reached the small cabin clearing and waited for Nathan to catch up. They both stopped and assessed the structure. "Doesn't look bad for being abandon," John said.

"Yeah, well, as long as it keeps us dry," Nathan said. "Let's go look inside."

Nathan stepped up on the porch, depressed the black thumb latch, and let the cabin door swing open.

They slowly walked in and cautiously looked around.

The old trapper's cabin had been built by Pat Galverson in his early days as the owner of Brown Airways. The cabin was constructed of two-by-eights Galverson had flown in himself on his own plane, and it had been built over the course of one summer. The inside consisted of one large room measuring twenty-four feet wide by thirty-five feet long, with an open truss ceiling. There was a window on each side of the cabin door, and one on each of the three remaining walls. The original intent was for the cabin to be a hunting and fishing vacation post. It turned out to be Pat

Galverson's final home as he fled from the harassment he received in Tear Falls and the embarrassment over his bankrupt business.

Nathan and John began to move about the cabin, the sound of their hiking boot footsteps echoing off the walls.

"Not much here," John said as he examined an old wood stove in the corner and looked at a peg coat rack on the wall.

"At least we have a table with four chairs, and I guess, a rocking chair," Nathan said, pulling the back of the rocking chair and setting it in motion.

"Well, all I care about is the roof doesn't leak," John said, looking up at the ceiling.

"Soon find out," Nathan replied. He took off his pack and placed it on the table, along with his gun case.

John took off his pack and balanced it on one of the wooden chairs. He untied his portable tape player, set it on the table, and turned on the radio.

"Get some weather reports," he said.

Nathan walked over to the front of the cabin and closed the door. It swung shut, rattling the two pictures hanging on the inside.

Nathan peered closer at them. "John...come here."

"Hold on," John said. "Here comes the 10:30 news. They'll report the weather."

Nathan turned back to his brother. "John...! Come here!"

John turned down the radio and came to the door. "What! What are you looking at?"

Nathan pointed at the top picture, which was of four men standing on a dock and holding fishing gear. A Brown Airways float plane was tied up to the dock behind them.

"Is that not Uncle Rick? The second guy to the right with the brown leather jacket on!"

"Holy shit. You are right!" John said. He looked at the other three men in the picture. "And that guy on the end. The older-looking guy. That's his old boss at Brown Airways. What's his name…Mr. Galverson!"

Nathan looked down at the second picture, which was of a man standing in front of a cabin. "That's gotta be Mr. Galverson in front of this cabin. Must have been when it was first built!"

Nathan looked at John. "The old trapper is Galverson? The trapper who found the plane in the book?"

John took a few steps back toward the table. "Oh fuck."

"What?" Nathan asked.

"That's why Chad DeMello thought Dad knew more about the gold. Chad, his dad, his uncle, they know the trapper is Galverson! Uncle Rick's old boss!"

John sat down at the table and rubbed his face with both hands. He looked back up at Nathan. "I knew Dad wasn't telling us something."

"Okay, Mr. Conspiracy. You don't know that for sure," Nathan replied as he sat down across from John.

"Nah, Dad knew. He just doesn't want to talk about it. Any of it!" John said. He pushed his chair out, walked over to one of the windows, and looked out. "Now what do we do?"

"Do? About what?" Nathan asked.

John turned back to his brother. "Nathan! Now I am convinced the DeMellos think we know where the gold is! How do you know they didn't follow us up here! Maybe they are going to go after Dad!"

"Okay, now you're really getting paranoid," Nathan said. He looked up to the ceiling to the sound of raindrops hitting the roof. He stood up, opened the top part of his pack, and threw John a can of beans. "Let's make lunch and relax. We'll wait out this rain. I can imagine the DeMellos, and Dad, are nice and dry at home, watching a baseball game on TV."

# Chapter Twenty-Three

# C.C.

"That's it!" Chad yelled from the cab of his dad's pickup truck. "Their red truck!"

Marty DeMello slammed on the brakes hard enough to cause the truck to sway on the wet gravel road. He reversed and looked at the back of Nathan's truck. "You sure that's it?"

"Yup! Has the Boston Bruins sticker on it. That's their truck."

David DeMello leaned forward in his seat on the other side of Chad and looked at his brother. "Why don't you go up a bit and park. No use letting them know we are here, in case they come back to their truck."

"Good idea," Marty said. He put the truck back in drive and drove up another hundred feet. To conceal the truck from view, he pulled it in as close to the ditch as he could without getting stuck.

David looked out his window. "Fucking rain! This supposed to last all day?"

"Supposed to drizzle all weekend," Marty said. "But someone told me there is a cabin up here that could keep us all dry!" he added with a laugh as he got out of the truck.

All three DeMellos put on green raincoats over black rain pants and then slipped on rubber boots. Marty and David reached into the back of the truck, took out their large backpacks, and strapped them on, while Chad pulled out a small grey pack.

"What's that? That your pack for school!" David teased.

"Don't need anything more!" Chad said. He pulled his coat up to reveal a large hunting knife strapped to one side of his belt and a small hatchet on the other side. "I've got enough trapping wire, fishing line, and anything else I need in my pack to last months. Anything else I need, I make!"

David looked over at Marty. "What have you been teaching this boy? Hockey or Mr. Bushman?"

"Hey, don't knock it!" Marty said. "He's read every book there is on how to survive in the bush." He reached into the back of the truck and grabbed three rifles. He handed one to Chad and one to his brother. "Besides, he'll be able to save your sorry ass in case there is that nuclear war you keep talking about."

Marty turned and started walking back towards Nathan and John's parked truck. "C'mon it's one o'clock. I want to be at that cabin by two!"

Chad looked at the cabin through some trees and then back at his dad and uncle. "Well, at least it's stopped raining." He put out his hand. "What do we do now? Just go knock on the door?"

David looked at his watch. "It is nearly 2:30, and we have been here at least fifteen minutes. I don't see anybody moving around in there. Chad, why don't you go take a peek in one of the windows, but keep your head down."

Chad walked a wide route through the bush and came to stand about ten feet from a side window of the cabin. He looked back at his dad and uncle for a sign.

"Go!" his dad whispered while directing Chad forward with his hand.

Chad crouched and moved up to the window. He stepped on a stump and looked inside.

"All clear!" he yelled, waving.

Marty, Chad, and David made their way to the front of the cabin. They stepped up onto the porch, and David opened the cabin door. "Anybody home?" he yelled out. "Nope, doesn't look like it." He held the door open for Marty and Chad. "C'mon in, guys!" he said with a smile.

Chad walked over to check out the stove. He picked up an empty can. "Beans!" he said. "What a bunch of wusses!"

"Hey, put that down, boy! They don't need to know anyone's been here," David said.

Marty looked at Nathan's pack, which was lying on the table with the top zipper undone. He moved the flap with the tip of his gun barrel to look inside. "I don't see nothing worth snooping for right now. No maps and no gold bars."

"We should go looking for them. Hunt them down like moose!" Chad said, laughing.

"Fuck no!" David said as he looked up at the wet spots on the ceiling. "We want to rob them, not kill 'em." He turned back to Marty. "Let's go set up camp at that clearing about twenty minutes back. We'll do a quick check on them tonight, but I figure they're still looking. We'll just pay them a little visit in the morning and ask them where the gold is."

***

Nathan and John returned to the cabin by six o'clock, just in time to have the rain resume its slow drizzle.

John took off his raincoat and hung it up on the wall. He walked over, sat in the rocking chair and slouched. "Well, can't say we are not getting some exercise," he said, rocking the chair. "How far do you think we walked today?"

"Looking at the map," Nathan said, "I would say we covered four square miles?"

John stood up and walked over to where Nathan was looking at the map. "Sometimes I wish Dad did know where the gold is. We're not even making a dent!"

"Hey, we may get lucky," Nathan said. He moved his pack from the table over to near the wood stove and pulled out a small frying pan, bread, and hotdogs. "Fried hotdogs?" he asked. "Got some ketchup packs!"

"I'm in!" John replied.

The boys finished off their dinner and turned on the radio to get Sunday's weather report. They listened to a forecast, which predicted steady rain for the entire next day.

"Can't get a break, can we?" John said.

"Nope," Nathan said with a smile. "But I think I have something to ease the pain." He stood up and went over to his pack. He pulled out a bottle of rye and showed it to John. "Canadian Club, baby!"

"Hey, where did you get that?" John asked, laughing.

Nathan brought the bottle over to the table, along with two plastic mugs. He set a mug in front of John and began to fill it. "There is this place in Tear Falls called the liquor store. You might have heard of it."

"Easy," John said. "Let me get my bottle of Coke." John went over to his own pack and brought back a small plastic Coke bottle. He topped off his own mug and did the same with his brother's.

Nathan raised his mug. "Yup, it's nice to be nineteen!"

"Does me good," John said, raising his mug.

John relaxed by leaning on the table and resting his chin on his two stacked fists. He looked at the half-empty bottle of rye. "That didn't take long."

"Nope," Nathan replied, leaning back in his chair and putting his feet up at the end of the table.

John stared straight ahead. "So, let me get this straight. Uncle Rick was trying to fly a plane full of stolen gold to Mexico, but something went wrong. He tries to land on Yars Lake, where he knows his old boss lives. His old boss reports finding the plane but no gold. The DeMellos think Dad knows where the gold is because he is Uncle Rick's friend. So they think Galverson took the gold from the plane and hid it somewhere, and somehow Dad knows where. But the Stinson Mine says they recovered the gold, and Dad says that, too. Galverson dies or disappears, but there is no mention of him being someone who might have taken the gold. Not the police, not Dad, not even in Chris Berts' book."

"Thanks for the Coles Notes, Columbo," Nathan said. "But what, may I ask, little brother, is your point?"

John looked over at Nathan. "Well, someone's got to be wrong. Someone's lying somewhere."

Nathan moved over and sat down in the chair directly across from John. He picked up the bottle of rye and struggled to refill their mugs without spilling. "Or it's all just one big bullshit game of Connect Four. We just have to make sure we are the winners!" He stood up from his chair, raised his mug, and downed his rye.

John smiled and then abruptly twisted his head. "Did you hear something?"

"Like what?" Nathan replied, steadying himself with two hands on the chair back. "Like Bigfoot?" he said, grinning.

"Like something outside. A thump or something."

"Nope. But why don't we listen to some tunes!" Nathan put his hands to the table to support himself. "What tape you got in this broom...this boombox anyway?"

John went over to look out the window of the cabin, struggling to see anything in the dark environs of the woods. "Toronto," he called back to Nathan.

"Toronto? The city?" Nathan laughed, hitting multiple buttons and causing the tape to do everything but play.

"The band!" John replied. "You'll like them." He turned back to Nathan. "Are we going to find that gold?"

"Who gives a shit!" Nathan replied. He finally hit the play button, and the cassette player started playing loud music. "But we're not going to find the DeMellos either!" he yelled with a smile. "Let's finish that bottle!"

Chapter Twenty-Four

# WOULD NEVER HAVE MADE IT

Kristen sat up in bed wearing a white muscle shirt and shivered. She looked over at the sound of the phone ringing on the bedside table and eyed the red LED stick icons on the clock forming 8:10 a.m.

*On a Sunday?* she thought as she picked up the phone. "Hello?"

"Mrs. Tonkin?"

"Yes."

"It's Sergeant Singh from the O.P.P. Can I speak to your husband, Milt?"

"Yes, of course!"

She nudged Milt. "It's for you," she whispered.

Milt propped himself up and took the phone. "Hello?"

"Milt, it's Rujoy Singh. Sergeant Singh. Can you come down to the detachment by nine this morning?"

Milt looked over at the LED clock. "Yeah, sure. Can you tell me what for? What's this is all about?"

"I looked into that Biggs disappearance like you asked. We have come up with some interesting information. We would like to discuss it with you as soon as possible."

"On my way," Milt replied. "See you at nine."

He handed the phone back to Kristen and sat up on the side of the bed.

"I think your little conversation with Carol Biggs might have paid off. Singh says he might have some new information. They want me to come down to the station to discuss it."

"Good, but be careful, Milt with what you say."

Milt turned back to Kristen. "You didn't just say that." He stood up, picked up his pants off the back of a chair, and started pulling them on. "Kristen, you were the one that told me to go there in the first place!"

"I know. To get them to do their job. Not for you to be part of it," she replied.

Milt took a shirt out of the closet. "Kristen, I'm going down there because I'm already a part of it. If this is headed where I think it's headed, the police may be the least of our worries!"

Kristen watched as Milt headed out of the bedroom to the kitchen. She heard the noise of a coffee pot, a microwave warming, and the slamming of the front door. She got up out of bed and looked out the window in time to see Milt driving away in the rain.

Milt pulled into the police parking lot and sat in his truck as he finished his coffee, hoping the rain would let up.

The front door of the station opened, and a man with stained-orange coveralls and black and grey tangled hair stepped out. The man made a run for his truck to avoid the rain, cursing as he stepped into water-filled potholes.

"What the fuck?" Milt said out loud. "What the hell is he doing here?"

He ducked down as Paul Rocelli drove by and out of the parking lot.

Milt got out of his truck and ran through the rain to the station. He opened the door and entered the lobby to see the familiar face of Constable Marsh behind the counter.

"Hello, Mr. Tonkin," Marsh said, placing his pen down. "Sergeant Singh's been waiting for you."

Milt looked over through Singh's office window. "Who is the blonde?"

"That's Sergeant Corbinsky. She's from a detachment down south. But go on in! You're not interrupting."

"Why do women in uniform always look so good, Marsh?"

"You're welcome to ask her, Mr. Tonkin," Marsh said, picking up his pen and going back to his paperwork.

Milt walked over and tapped on the glass window of Singh's door. Singh motioned for him to come in.

"Hello, Milt!" Singh said. "Like you to meet Sergeant Debra Corbinsky. She's with the provincial special crimes investigations unit."

"Hello, Mr. Tonkin," Sergeant Corbinsky said, extending her hand and smiling.

"Hello," Milt replied, shaking Corbinsky's hand for an inordinate length of time.

"Have a seat, Milt," Singh said, breaking up Milt's awkward greeting.

Milt sat down and turned his attention back to Singh. He could hear Kristen's parting words from the morning echoing in his head.

"Look, I don't know anything more than I told you the first time I was in. I was just pointing out what was said by a friend. Like a tip or something for you guys."

"Relax, Milt," Singh said. "It was a good tip. Now let us show you what we found. Sergeant Corbinsky, do you want to explain?"

Corbinsky opened a brown file folder on the desk and turned it around to show Milt. "This is the file of the original police report of Randy Biggs's death from 1972. It was prepared by Sergeant McIntyre, the detachment commander at the time."

Milt took a few minutes to read through the report. He saw statements outlining the cause of death as drowning and the location being Fenny Lake. There were also a number of pictures taken of the area where the accident took place.

Milt looked up. "So? This report agrees it was a drowning."

Corbinsky picked out one of the pictures and handed it to Milt. "I want you to take a good look at this picture. You've lived here all your life. You tell me what's wrong with that picture taken the day after Biggs fell through."

Milt looked at it. "Well, I see some broken ice in an open area of water. Snow around it looks pretty slushy. Typical of signs there might be bad ice there."

He started to hand the picture back to Corbinsky but stopped and took a closer look. "This happened the middle of January."

"Yes," Corbinsky said.

"It's averaging thirty below at night and twenty below during the day."

Corbinsky crossed her arms. "Exactly!"

"Shit!" Milt said, looking at Corbinsky. "That water should be frozen over even if Biggs did fall through!"

"Yes, it should be!" Corbinsky replied. "And that's not the only thing that's out of place in these pictures. Look at this one."

Milt took another picture out of Corbinsky hand and looked at a wide shot of the lake. "I don't see anything in this picture other than a snowy lake."

Corbinsky leaned over and pointed to the very top of the picture, to two barely visible small trees in the middle of the lake.

"Now, what would two small trees be doing in the middle of the lake?" she asked.

Milt looked up. "Runway markers!"

"Yes," Corbinsky said, leaning back in her chair. "Guess the person taking the pictures was not too particular on what was in the background. There is no marked runway on Fenny Lake."

Milt handed the picture back to Corbinsky. "So, it's all true, then. Biggs was murdered! By the DeMellos! And this report. This report is a coverup?"

Corbinsky closed up the file. "Mr. Tonkin, we have long suspected Biggs's death was a homicide. Sergeant McIntyre worked here before Singh. He was a good man, but he was an alcoholic. All the files around here when he was working are a mess. We don't believe he had anything to do with this other than just taking what others handed him. The easy way out. We doubt he even looked at these pictures."

"Well, that's crazy!" Milt looked at Corbinsky and back to Singh. "What are you going to do about it? Why haven't you arrested the DeMellos or that Fritz guy!"

"Calm down, Milt," Singh said. "We'll explain."

He went around his desk and opened the office door. "Marsh!" he called out. "Three waters!"

"Right away, sir," Marsh replied.

He returned with three bottles of water and set them on the desk.

Milt opened a bottle and took a long drink. "Okay, there...I'm calm. Now can you tell me? Why hasn't someone arrested these guys? And while we are at it, can you please tell me why Paul Rocelli was here, my best friend's old boss?"

Corbinsky looked at Singh and back to Milt. She stood up, walked over to the office window, and looked out at the lobby.

"Mr. Tonkin, do you know why Randy Biggs was murdered?" she asked as she turned her head back to face Milt. "And let there be no doubt, he was murdered."

"He screwed up in having that Fritz guy's plane stolen with gold. I don't know. How much are those planes worth? Hundred thousand plus? Who knows what can set a guy off?"

Corbinsky walked back around Singh's desk. "It's drugs, Mr. Tonkin. The gold your friend stole has nothing to do with it." She picked up the Biggs file. "This Fritz guy you mention, Fritz Rinestein, who is in this report, is a major drug dealer. Even all that gold your friend tried to steal with Fritz's plane is a drop in the bucket compared to his drug operations."

"So, Randy Biggs..."

"Was working for him, Milt," Singh said. "He was a small-time dealer who could expose the whole operation. The DeMellos? They're Fritz's strongmen, but they are only dangerous because

Fritz is dangerous. It's all about image to Fritz. He'll do anything to keep it."

Milt looked at the ceiling and took a deep breath. "Okay, so, what you are telling me is this is all even way bigger than Randy Biggs being murdered. It's some fucking huge drug-smuggling ring? And why are you telling me all this? I knew nothing about Rick stealing the plane, and I know nothing about this drug smuggling!"

"Milt, you asked why Paul Rocelli was in here," Singh said leaning forward. "The simple answer is we need help. We need help from someone who can get the DeMellos talking. We can't solve the Biggs murder, and we can't arrest the DeMellos or bring Fritz Rinestein's drug operation down without evidence."

"Oh, and let me guess," Milt said. "Rocelli said no. Because maybe, just maybe, he might wind up like Biggs?"

"'Bad for business' is actually what he said," Singh said leaning back.

"Great! That's real great, Singh." Milt stood up from his chair, walked to the far corner of the room, and turned to face the two sergeants. He brushed his top lip several times with his hand.

"How big?"

"How big what?" Singh asked.

Milt came back and put his hands on Singh's desk. "How big is this drug smuggling, Singh? What are we talking about here! Northern Ontario? Out to major cities?"

"Across Ontario," Corbinsky interjected. "Maybe Canada."

Milt slowly looked up at Corbinsky. "Okay, now that is nuts. That's fucking nuts! Tear Falls is at the heart of a countrywide drug operation? That doesn't add up!" He reached for his water and took another drink.

"It actually does, Mr. Tonkin," Corbinsky said, looking down at her notes. "Do you know what an A7 is, Mr. Tonkin?"

"Never heard of it," Milt replied, looking over at Singh with a puzzled look. Singh raised his eyebrows.

"It's a security clearance for airports. An A7 is the highest level a civilian aviation company can obtain coming and going from Canadian airports. It is vetted by the RCMP through an application supported by local police. Fritz's company was granted an A7 with the help of the Tear Falls police, with the help of McIntyre."

Corbinsky took out a piece of paper from an open briefcase on Singh's desk and handed it to Milt. "That's an A7. It may have been issued for the Tear Falls Airport, but it allowed Fritz to fly to any airport in Canada and bypass normal security."

Milt studied the embossed sealed paper and looked up. "So, Fritz had a free pass to smuggle drugs to any town, any city in Canada as long as he had this A7?"

"Precisely," Corbinsky said. "So, you see, small towns offer perfect cover for illicit drug dealing if you know the right people. Make the right friends. Nobody suspects a good citizen like Fritz Rinestein. Tear Falls is a great place to run things. Until you have a plane crash, of course."

Milt sat down and placed his hand on his forehead as he stared at the floor. He looked back up. "So, Fritz is still in business. You haven't shut him down even after everything you know and all these years."

"We have disrupted his operations, and we actually think it's having an effect," Corbinsky said. "Arrested a few of his people involved in selling his drugs, but Fritz is very good at insulating himself even when someone under him goes to jail. He also changes his means of smuggling."

"You mean no more planeloads of drugs coming into Tear Falls escorted by the police," Milt said with a smirk.

Corbinsky reached down to the floor, picked up an object, and placed it on Singh's desk. "You are right, Mr. Tonkin. He lost his A7 with the crash, but this is how we think he is doing it now."

Milt read the glass object's engraved label. He looked up in shock. "Where did you get that?"

"It was confiscated as part of drug seizure from a moving truck at the Canada-US border," Corbinsky replied. "But we think Fritz is using them all over to smuggle. Drug dogs can't detect what they can't smell."

"You seem disturbed, Milt," Singh said. "What is it? You recognize it?"

Milt nervously rubbed the arms of his chair. "Fuck, that's an air tight. It's from fucking Rennet."

"From Rennet?" Singh asked. "How do you know that, Milt?"

Milt reached over and picked up the gallon-sized glass container. "I can't say for sure, but these have been going missing at the mine. There is a guy..." Milt stopped himself. "There have been reports of these things being taken from the Rennet Mine lab."

"Well, I would say that is hardly a coincidence, then," Singh said. "We knew they weren't coming from the local hardware store."

"Jesus Christ," Milt said under his breath as he put the container back on the desk. "Fucking Campbell..."

"What was that?" Corbinsky asked.

"Nothing, nothing," Milt replied. "This guy at the... I mean... Okay...the DeMellos. Can we just talk about why the DeMellos are so interested in the gold from the plane crash after all these years when it was recovered by the Stinson Mine? Or is this some other gold cartel thing I should know about before you ask me to talk to two murders?"

"The gold is payback, Mr. Tonkin," Corbinsky said, "to their boss for the lost plane but, more importantly, for the unwanted attention the crash brought to the drug smuggling. We think the DeMellos are at risk to this very day for what happened." Corbinsky motioned to Singh, who took out another file and handed it to her. "You know your friend wouldn't have even come close to making it to Mexico when he did steal the plane?"

Milt drew his head back, and his eyes narrowed. "What do you mean he wouldn't have made it? Rick was a damn good pilot! Just ran into some bad weather. Bad luck, that's all!"

"No, it was more than bad weather. More than bad luck. You see, your friend Rick didn't have enough fuel. Even though he thought he did. Those extra tanks Fritz had on that plane had false bottoms to store drugs. We found all that out when we recovered the plane. He would have made it halfway, maybe three-quarters, but he would have crashed eventually or have been forced to land in the U.S., where he would have been arrested." Corbinsky dropped the file on the desk. "It's all here."

Milt sat forward. "You have a file on everything?" He asked, his eyes wide. "So, what about the gold, then? You still haven't answered that."

Corbinsky turned to Singh. "I think it's time."

Singh nodded in agreement.

"Milt, we need to know now if you would consider helping us out before we go any further. We have probably told you too much already. Your friend Rick committed a crime, but in doing so, he exposed a network of drug smuggling, corruption, and, as we suspect, murder, not only in Tear Falls, but probably in a number of small towns across the country." Singh looked up at Corbinsky, and she signalled for him to continue.

"Would you consider being an informant for the Ontario Provincial Police?"

Milt took off his glasses and placed them on his lap, folding the arms back and forth. He looked up. "You want me to wear a wire? That's basically what you're asking me to do. Maybe fake that I know where the gold is up at Yars Lake even though it is long gone. You know, I tell my kids to stay away from the DeMellos. I tell my wife how rotten they are, and now I'm supposed to become the DeMello twins' best friend?" Milt smiled. "You guys don't ask for much, do you?"

"You wouldn't have to wear a wire. We have other ways," Corbinsky said. "We would protect your job at the Rennet Mine. We would also make sure you and your family were protected, and we would pay you."

"I don't know. I just… This is a lot to think about. I feel for Carol Biggs. I know the DeMellos deserve prison. Fuck, and this Fritz guy. I don't even know who this Fritz guy is, and he is ruining my town."

"Just think about it, Milt," Singh said. "But we ask you don't discuss the details of this meeting with your wife or anyone else. It's that sensitive. We'll wait to hear from you. In the meantime, we have other reasons to pay the DeMellos a visit this weekend. Always good to keep tabs on those guys." Singh stood up and came around his desk. "But whatever you decide, we're eventually going to get them. They will slip up sooner or later."

Milt stood up and let out a deep breath. "Yeah! Sooner or later."

Singh squeezed Milt's shoulder, and the two men shook hands. "Thanks for coming in, Milt!"

"I really don't think I had a choice," Milt replied.

"Well, we appreciate it just the same, Mr. Tonkin," Corbinsky said.

She reached out and shook Milt's hand. "You've already been a big help," she said, smiling.

"Yeah, well, it's been quite a Sunday morning, hasn't it."

Singh pointed up to the clock on the wall. "It's only a little past ten, Milt. You still have most of the morning left."

"Yeah, you're right. What time does the NearNorth serve liquor again?"

## Chapter Twenty-Five

# FRENCH TOAST

"Give me those binoculars. Fuck, what time is it?" David DeMello asked Chad, taking the binoculars away from him.

"It's 10:30," Chad said. "I'm telling you, they are still sleeping. I even went up to the window to take a look."

Marty came up to the other two. "What the fuck is this, a stakeout? Why haven't they left yet?"

David took another look with the binoculars. "Could be they are just pussies in the rain." He gave the binoculars back to Chad. "I say we go knock on the door."

"It's been long enough," Marty said. "We can't waste any more time on these shitheads. Let's go and let ourselves in."

"Agreed!" David said.

Chad crouched down with his gun and started toward the front door, rain spattering off his backside.

Marty and David looked at each other, smiling. "What the fuck are you doing, Chad?" David said. "This isn't some army raid."

Marty and David walked up and past Chad with their guns slung over their shoulders. They stepped up on the porch, and David pounded on the door. He turned to Chad. "We are just here to get out of the rain. Is that too much to ask?"

***

Milt came home to a note from Kristen on the kitchen table. She had gone to the store and was meeting Tracy afterwards at the Abby for coffee. There was leftover chicken in the fridge for him if he wanted to make a sandwich. Milt opened the fridge door and looked at the chicken. He reached past it, took out a jug of cold water, and poured himself a glass. Then he walked into their bedroom, where he took a shoebox down from the closet shelf and spilled the contents on the bed. He separated out a small piece of rolled-up paper, opened it up, and sat on the edge of the bed. Placing his fingers on either side of the paper, he took a deep breath, and started a slow rip. He got a quarter of the way through before he exhaled and stopped. His eyes fixated on the sketched picture within. He stood, carefully folded it up, and put it in his back pocket.

He turned his attention to the rest of the newspaper articles on the bed and hurriedly began to sort. He could find no information on Fritz Rinestein being the owner of the crashed Cessna, as Corbinsky had suggested. There was no mention of drug smuggling or any suspicion Randy Biggs's death was anything other than a coincidental tragic accident a week later.

He spotted a collection of newspaper photographs bound together with a clasped paperclip. He picked them up and sat down in the bedroom chair. He read the headline at the bottom of the top picture: "Police Are Golden To The Stinson Mine." The picture was of a smiling Sergeant McIntyre beside the then Stinson Mine manager at a 1972 press conference on the recovery of the gold. His eyes were drawn to the sergeant's smile, and he could hear Corbinsky's words about McIntyre always taking the easy way out. He thought of Carol Biggs giving up on any justice for her son's murder and Fritz Rinestein thinking he had got away with it. He stood up, placed the picture back on the bed, and picked up another of the mangled wreckage of Rick's stolen Cessna on Yars

Lake. *He would have never made it,* he said to himself. He looked up to the ceiling. *This is where we go better, my friend!*

***

"Somebody's at the door!" Nathan said as he sat up from the floor in his sleeping bag and rubbed his eyes.

"What?" John asked, sitting up in his own sleeping bag. "What time is it?"

"Shit, it's twenty after eleven. Might be someone checking to see if they can use the cabin."

The boys heard the noise again. Nathan got up and looked out the side window near the door but was unable to recognize the DeMellos with their hoods up.

"Looks like three guys. Three wet guys!"

John stood up. "Well, just tell them no vacancy."

Nathan went over to the door and opened it. "Hey, there is no—"

"Good morning, Tonkins!" David DeMello said as he stepped into the cabin, followed by his brother and Chad. David put his hood down, walked over to the table, and looked up at the ceiling and around the cabin. "Nice and dry in here."

Nathan and John looked at Chad, who stared back, smiling at their shocked faces.

Marty walked over to the wood stove and felt for any heat off the top with his hand. "You boys should keep this stove going all night. Then you wouldn't have to be in those sweaters and sweatpants you're wearing right now."

"Yeah, good idea," John said. "Uh…we're only here one more day, if you need the cabin. I know it's been raining most of the weekend, and it's hard to stay dry."

"I don't think we need the cabin. Don't plan on staying long," David said. He took his gun off his shoulder, walked over to the rocking chair, and sat down. He placed his gun across the arms

220

and gently rocked the chair. Chad went over to stand at the door, and Marty went and stood by a window.

"You boys want to tell us what you are doing up here? Because we know why we are here. Maybe we can help each other out. You know, like a team." David pointed at two table chairs with the tip of his gun. "Have a seat, and let's have ourselves a little conversation."

***

Milt looked at his watch. It was 11:30 a.m., and he had been sitting by the phone in the living room for close to an hour. He looked at Singh's card on the table and dialled the Tear Falls police number, promising himself not to hang up for a third time.

"Ontario Provincial Police," Marsh said.

"Constable Marsh?"

"Yes. Who's this?"

"It's Milt Tonkin. Is Sergeant Singh in?"

"He was just about to go home for the day, but let me check." Milt waited and heard a click.

"Sergeant Singh."

"Sergeant. It's Milt."

"Yes, Milt. Didn't expect a call back so soon. What can I do for you?"

"I've decided I will help you out. It's the least I can do for Randy Biggs's mother and my friend Rick. And the DeMellos and this Fritz Rinestein, wouldn't mind seeing them leave Tear Falls for good."

"Couldn't agree more, Milt. You're doing the right thing. We'll need you to come back to the station. Any chance you can do that Tuesday morning, say about 8:30 a.m.?"

"Work afternoons, so that works."

"Perfect. I'll let Sergeant Corbinsky know, and we'll see you then."

"One more thing before you go, Sergeant."

"Yes, and please call me Rujoy, Milt. I think we can do away with the formalities at this point."

"The gold. The whole reason you think the DeMellos will talk to me. How am I going to make up a story they'll believe?"

"Galverson," Singh said. "I think you have at least thought about that, Milt. And to answer your next question, yes, we believe he took it from the plane. It was never lost on the police, the connection between Rick crashing on Yars Lake and his old boss having a cabin there."

"So, are you saying the book is true and the police and Stinson are liars? Tell me, Singh, is everybody corrupt in this town?"

"I wouldn't say corrupt, Milt. Convenient omission of the truth, maybe. It was just another so-called official report by McIntyre," Singh said. "The Stinson Mine just told him they found it. Gave him all the credit and gave themselves more time to search for the gold without all the attention."

"But as far as you know, they never found it," Milt said.

"Not one bar has been recovered as far as we know," Singh replied. "We have our theories that Galverson hid it over at the Davidson mine. That's an old silver mine. There are shafts mined into the side of rock faces, and fifteen-foot trenches dug out all over the place. He could have stashed it anywhere."

"Okay, but this is just another theory about Galverson. No different than the Torrison treasure book theory it fell out of the plane or Rick pushed it out."

"True. We are not certain. But looking for the gold is not exactly high on our priority list, Milt. The Stinson Mine can take care of that one on their own, and they have insurance. Our focus is on solving the Biggs murder and shutting down Fritz's drug smuggling. And as for Galverson, nobody really knows how or why he went missing."

"DeMellos?"

"That, we don't know, but…"

"You would like to find out. I think I'm getting the hang of this, Singh."

"Every little bit helps, Milt."

"Yeah…well, I guess we can talk about all of this on Tuesday. All I need to know now is how to plant the seed with the DeMellos about Galverson and go from there."

"Won't be much of a plant, Milt. The DeMellos already think Galverson was involved. In fact, they are up at Yars Lake this weekend looking for the gold. They are desperate to pay Fritz back by getting his reputation back even after all these years."

Milt sat up on the couch. "What did you say?"

"I said the DeMellos are desperate to pay Fritz back."

"No, before that. The DeMellos are up at Yars Lake this weekend? How do you know that?"

"It's no big deal, Milt. They have probably looked for the gold up there a million times."

"Singh! How do you know they are up at Yars Lake?"

"Constable Marsh knocked on Marty DeMello's door this morning, and his wife told him. Other matters, Milt."

Milt bolted up. "I gotta go, Singh!"

"Milt, what's the matter? That's just routine police work."

"I gotta go!" Milt slammed down the receiver, rushed to the kitchen, and ran his finger down a list of numbers on a sheet of paper taped to the side of the cupboard. He found the Abby Cafe and punched in the number on the wall phone.

"Hello, Abby Cafe. Janice speaking."

"Janice! It's Mr. Tonkin. Milt Tonkin, John's dad! Is my wife still there?"

"Uh, yeah…I think so. Pretty busy. Let me see if I still have their bill."

Milt could hear the sounds of the restaurant as Janice placed the phone down. He brushed a bead of sweat off his forehead.

Janice picked up again. "Yeah, they must be still here because they had…let's see…yeah, it was an order of French toast, a—"

"Fuck the French toast!" Milt said.

"Well, the French Toast is not that bad, Mr. Tonkin. Are you okay? You sound stressed."

"No. Yes. I mean, I'm okay. Janice, listen to me. Can you just please go over to my wife's table and tell her to bring the truck home as soon as possible! I need it right away!"

"Yeah, sure. I will do that right now."

"Thank you."

Milt hung up the phone, took a key out of a side kitchen drawer, and rushed to the basement. He unlocked a large stand-up black locker and took out his hunting jacket. He inverted the sleeves, reversing the bright orange colour of the jacket to a green, and put it on. Then he grabbed a box of bullets, took out his rifle, and ran back upstairs.

## Chapter Twenty-Six

# MAP QUEST

"G rid search!" David DeMello grabbed John by the hair and pushed his head down to the map the boys had spread out on the table. "No more horseshit, boy. Tell us where your dad said to look for the gold! You must know something more than this!"

"We don't know anything more than this map!" John said. "He didn't tell us anything about where it is!"

"You're hurting him!" Nathan yelled. He took a step forward but was met by the stock of Marty DeMello's gun to the side of his gut. He collapsed to the floor with a groan.

Still holding John's head down, David looked behind him to see Nathan on the cabin floor. "You know, Marty, I think these boys still think we are fooling around. Seems they think keeping their dad's secret is worth it!" He reached behind the back of his jacket, pulled out a handgun, and put it to John's head. "You think it's worth it now, Tonkin! You think ending up out here dead is worth it to your old man!"

"We have another map!" Nathan yelled from the floor. "Don't kill him!"

Marty stepped over to Nathan and put the barrel of his rifle underneath the boy's chin. "What are you talking about. Another map. Where?"

"Let him go, and I will tell you!" Nathan said.

David took the gun away from John's head and pulled him up. He shoved him down in a chair and then walked over to Nathan and squatted in front of him with the pistol in his hand. "You better not be talking shit, boy."

"We have another map at the truck," Nathan said, trembling. "We forgot it there and were waiting for the rain to stop to go get it." John and Nathan exchanged glances.

"Want me to march one of them back, David?" Marty asked.

David stood up, walked back over to the table, and looked down at the map. "Nahh...that's not necessary. We have a perfectly good set of legs in Chad over there." He turned back to Nathan. "Where are the keys, and where is the map?"

"Truck keys are in my coat pocket on the wall," Nathan said. "The map is in, I think, the glove compartment. Or no, the hockey bag in the back. I should go with Chad."

David looked at Marty, and they both laughed. "You've been watching too many movies, Tonkin." He reached into Nathan's coat pocket, took out the keys to his truck, and threw them over to Chad.

"Go back to the truck and bring back the map. Or they better hope you bring it back!" David walked over to Nathan's pack, which was leaning against the wall, and unzipped the top. "Now, didn't I hear you boys bought a shitload of stuff at Frank Riley's store? There's got to be some rope in here somewhere."

\*\*\*

Milt glanced at his watch to see it was nearly noon. He looked up to see Kristen finally pulling into the driveway. She jumped out of the truck and ran through the pouring rain to the door. She opened it to see Milt in his jacket, waiting to meet her.

"Milt! What is going on?! They told me you wanted me back in a hurry. Is it Rick's mom?"

"It's the boys, Kristen. I have to go check on them!" Milt grabbed his gun from beside the door and went out to the truck. Kristen ran after him and stopped him as he opened the truck door. "What is wrong with the boys, Milt? Why the rush? You're scaring me!"

Milt looked at Kristen. Her curly brown hair had become flat and soaked. He was unsure if the drops of water on her face were rain or tears. "It's nothing, hon. Really. It's the weather. It's going…it's going to get worse! I just want them out of there."

"But they are alright?" she asked with reddened eyes.

Milt threw his rifle on the passenger seat and got in the truck. He put his hand on the door rest to close the door. "They're fine, hon. Everything is fine, but can you do me a favour? Call Oakey and ask him to meet me up at Yars Lake as soon as possible. He has a quad. Tell him the old trapper's cabin. The Davidson Mine!"

"Yes, I will call him."

Milt closed the truck door and rolled down the window. "And tell him to bring his gun. There are lots of bears up there! Just want to be safe!"

Kristen watched in the rain as Milt backed the truck out of the driveway. She heard the tires slip on the wet pavement as he drove away.

She ran back into the house, dried her face, and wiped her nose. She read Oakey's number off the cupboard sheet and picked up the phone.

"It's me, Oakey. Who are you?"

"Hi, Oakey. It's Kristen!"

"Oh, hi, Kristy! How are you?"

"I'm good, Oakey. Milt asked me to call you. He wants you to meet him up at Yars Lake as soon as possible."

"Really? In this weather?"

"He needs your help in getting our boys out of the bush before the weather gets worse. Asked if you can bring your quad up there."

"Yeah, that's no problem, Kristy. I'll go, but is all okay? You don't sound so good."

"I think so, Oakey. I'm just…well worried. He… If you can just go and meet him. He is going to look for them at the old trapper's cabin and Davidson Mine. Oh, and he says bring your gun for bears."

"I always bring my gun, Kristy."

"Thanks, Oakey! Milt always appreciates your help."

"For sure. I'll leave in a few minutes."

Kristen went to the cupboard and took out a wine glass. She poured herself a tall glass of white wine from a bottle in the fridge and went to sit down on the living room couch. She was determined to keep calm until Milt's return. She looked over at the side table and noticed Singh's card beside the phone and picked it up. She realized she had completely forgotten about Milt's meeting with Singh in her rush to get home and in her worry about the boys. She tapped the card on her knee a few times and looked at the number. She picked up the phone.

\*\*\*

Milt looked down at the odometer reading on his truck and judged he was close to the Yars Lake cut-off. He came around a corner on the Bitman logging road and spotted Nathan's red pickup. He pulled in beside his son's truck and jumped out, carrying his gun. He had just looked in the front and back of his son's truck when he heard a noise in the bush. He backed off and found cover in time to see Chad DeMello coming out of the forest.

"This fucking map better be here!" Chad said as he stopped and looked up at the falling rain from under his hood.

Chad took the keys out of his pocket and was about to open the driver-side door when he noticed Milt's truck on the other side. *What the hell?* he said to himself as walked around to take a closer look. He put his hand to the grill of Milt's truck and could feel the heat. He looked around. "Hey! Somebody else here? Anybody here!"

He turned back to Nathan's truck, opened the passenger door, and popped the glove compartment. He looked around the whole time to see if anyone was watching.

"Shit, there is nothing here," he said, throwing the glove compartment contents on the seat.

Milt watched as Chad moved from the passenger-side door, came around to the left side of the truck, and reached into the truck's cargo box.

Milt came out of the bushes and approached Chad from behind. He pointed his rifle at his back.

"Chad! What are you doing? Where are John and Nathan?"

Chad spun around, startled. "Oh, Mr. Tonkin. Hi. I'm here... I'm here to pick some stuff up for them!"

Milt walked closer. "Chad, where are my sons?"

"They're here," Chad said, looking nervously at the gun. "They're back at the cabin near the lake."

Milt looked at the bush and then back at Chad. "And where is your dad, your uncle? They around?"

"No, no," Chad said, trying to smile. "Mr. Tonkin, didn't Nathan and John tell you about this trip?"

"Tell me what?"

"I'm here with them. We are exploring together. My dad dropped me off. See, there are no other trucks around here." Chad motioned at the surroundings. "Can you put that gun down, Mr. Tonkin? You are really making me nervous!"

Milt pointed the gun barrel down and rested the gun on his forearm as he moved up to Chad. "You really think I'm going to buy that, Chad? We're going back down this trail to the cabin to see whether my sons agree with your story. How's that?"

"Okay, Mr. Tonkin. No problem. We can do that." Chad reached his right hand behind him, into the hockey bag, and gripped a two-foot-long piece of tent pole. He placed his left hand into his pocket and took out the truck keys. "I guess you can take these, then."

Milt looked down and reached out to take the keys. Chad took advantage of the moment of distraction and swung the heavy tent pole. It hit Milt's shoulder and deflected up against the side of his head, knocking him over and opening a large gash on his left temple.

"Fuck!" Milt yelled as he fell to the ground, holding his head. He blinked to see Chad coming at him to deliver another blow. He rolled, grabbed his dropped gun, and rolled back to point the gun up at Chad. "I'll shoot you, Chad! I'll shoot you dead!"

Chad paused above him, holding the pole, his hand shaking. He looked down to see blood and rain mixing into a stream across Milt's face. He backed up a few steps, his eyes dilated with fear.

"Put it down, Chad! Just put it down!"

Chad dropped the pole and ran.

Milt bolted up. "Chad...Chad! Come back here!"

As Chad ran across the road, he glanced back, expecting a chase. Milt watched as he stopped, turned on the other side of the road, and stared back through a curtain of rain. Both men appeared to make an effort to speak, but both stopped in anticipation of the other's words. Chad's face became expressionless. He turned and disappeared into the bush.

Milt could feel his head throbbing. He placed his hand to his left temple and removed it to see his fingers were covered in blood. He walked over to his truck, opened the passenger-side door, and pulled out a first aid kit from behind the seat. He sat in the passenger seat and closed the door. "Fuck..." he said, looking up at the roof of the truck, trying to direct the blood off his face. He opened up the first aid kit and applied a large Band-Aid to his head. He took a moment to take some deep breaths. His mind started to race. He now knew his boys were in real trouble, and he was unsure of whether he should wait for Oakey. He pressed the tape on the bandage, opened the door, and headed for the cabin.

***

David sat in the rocking chair, moving it slowly back and forth while his brother paced the floor and looked out the window.

"Will you relax, Marty!" he said. "He should be back in ten minutes or so." He looked over at Nathan and John, who were tied to two chairs at the table. "I mean, look at the Tonkin boys here. They look relaxed." He laughed.

Nathan looked at John and then back at David. "What if Chad can't find it?" he asked.

David jumped up from the rocking chair, surprising the boys with his unexpected rage. He walked over to Nathan and pointed his handgun at his head. "Oh, he'll find it, Tonkin. You better hope he finds it."

Marty interrupted, saying, "It's past two. Something's wrong." He looked out the window again.

David put his gun down, came over, and looked out the window on the other side of the door. "You know what? It looks like it's stopped fucking raining. Why don't you go down to the lake and get some water for coffee? I'll get this wood stove going. Shouldn't be much longer."

Marty went to his pack in the corner of the cabin and removed a canteen bottle. He looked back at David. "That's all the time we're giving them. A fucking coffee break!" he said as he headed out the door to the lake.

David placed his handgun in his back waistband and walked over to the wood stove. He opened up the front grate and picked up some small kindling beside the stove. "You boys better hope Chad returns soon," he said. He started to break the wood and whistle.

## Chapter Twenty-Seven

# SKETCHY

Milt came up to the edge of the bush near the cabin and stopped. He moved parallel to the cabin and slowly walked in a crouch to a side window. He looked in to see David DeMello putting wood into the stove with his back toward him. He turned his gaze to the middle of the room and made eye contact with Nathan and John. He put his finger to his lips as he watched their faces express surprise.

He crouched down again, moved around to the cabin front, and stepped up onto the front porch. He took another look through the door side window and once again made eye contact with the boys. He put his hand up and silently counted to three with his fingers and gave the boys a thumbs up. They both nodded back. Milt grabbed the door handle. He counted to three and threw open the door.

"Put your hands up, DeMello, or I'll shoot! Hands up and turn around!" he yelled, pointing the rifle.

David put his hands up and slowly turned around. "Milt! Take it easy there, buddy. Your boys are okay. They just got a bit unruly. I tied them up for their own good!"

"Shut up, DeMello! Shut the fuck up and move over to the back of the cabin!"

"Hey, anything you say, Milt." David walked back a few steps with his hands up. "Good?"

"Dad, he's got a gun!" Nathan yelled. "It's in his back belt!"

Milt looked at Nathan and then back at DeMello. "Throw your gun on the floor, DeMello. Throw it on the floor, or I swear I'll blow your fucking head off!"

David could see a trickle of blood leave the bandage on Milt's head and run down the side of his face. "You've got yourself a little head wound there, Milt. Maybe you are not thinking right."

"Shut up. Shut the fuck up and do what I say!"

David reached to the back of his jacket, took out the gun, and held the handle between two fingers. He looked past Milt to see his brother appear in the door entrance. He smiled at Milt. "Where do you want it, Milt?"

"Slide it across the floor!"

David slowly squatted down and slid the handgun towards Milt.

"Don't move!" Milt said. He was bending down to pick up the gun when he felt Marty DeMello's canteen come down on the back of his head.

***

Oakey pulled up along the ditch to see the three vehicles parked side by side in the off-road clearing. He rolled down the window. "Holy fuck," he said. "All this for some bad weather?"

He stopped his truck halfway on the shoulder and got out. He placed his rifle over his camouflage rain jacket, put down the ramps on the truck, and unloaded his quad. He throttled the quad and raced up the road a hundred feet, at which point he came upon the DeMello truck. *Another truck?* he thought. He slowed down and looked into the back of the truck box, where he spotted some hockey sticks. He stopped, reached in, and picked one up. He read the name written in black marker on the stick: "Marty DeMello." His heart rate immediately went up.

He threw the stick back into the truck, spun the quad around on the wet road, and headed back toward the other three parked vehicles. He raced past Nathan's and Milt's trucks and the O.P.P cruiser and headed up the trail toward the cabin and Davidson Mine.

***

Marty DeMello threw water from the canteen on Milt's face. "Rise and shine there, Tonkin!"

Milt sat up, wiped the water away from his dazed face, and looked up at a smiling Marty and David DeMello.

"C'mon, Marty. Let's get our rescue hero over to a chair and tie him up. Make it a family affair!" David said with a laugh.

Marty stood in front of a seated Milt, whose hands were bound behind the chair. He looked at his bandage. "Looks like your head's been taking a beating today, Tonkin. How'd you get that gash on the side of your head?"

"Hit by... Fell on a rock. Fell on a wet rock on the way over here," Milt said.

He leaned his head back and stretched his neck. He squinted his eyes from the pain that was now radiating throughout his head and down his body.

"Are you alright, Dad?" John asked.

"I'm fine, son." Milt looked over at both DeMellos. "Let my sons go. They know nothing about where the gold is." He bowed his head toward the floor in more pain. "But I do!"

David DeMello joined Marty in front of Milt. "Finally, a Tonkin who knows something. Keep talking, Tonkin. You have the map with you?"

"There is no map," Milt said, looking back up at the twins.

David gave Nathan and John a hard stare. "Knew these boys were fucking liars. Must be what is taking Chad so long."

Milt noticed David looking at his boys. "No, I did give them a map! Just not the right one," he struggled to say through the pain. He looked over at his two sons. "Sorry about that, boys."

David raised his handgun up and pointed it at Milt.

"Don't shoot!" Nathan yelled. "Don't shoot my dad!"

David looked at Nathan. "I'm not going to shoot your dad, boy! But I will shoot one of you if he doesn't start making sense!" He looked back at Milt. "How about it, Tonkin? The map. Where is it?" He swung the gun to point at Nathan and pulled the hammer back while still looking at Milt.

"It's at the Davidson Mine!" Milt yelled out. "I don't have a map, but I'm pretty sure I know where it is."

David put the gun down and sat on the corner of the table. "Now we are getting somewhere!"

"Galverson, old man Galverson, took Rick's guns from the plane when it crashed. He gave them to me a year later, a rifle and a shotgun. I gave the rifle away, but when I went to clean the shotgun, there was a paper in the barrel. A sketch of a mine shaft. I didn't think it meant anything, but it must be where he put the gold!" Milt said, breathing heavily.

"You never—"

"Shut up, John!" Milt snapped. "You boys didn't need to know anything…any of this!" Then, to David, he said, "The sketch is in my back pocket! Take it! You can find the gold yourself!"

Marty laughed. "Oh fuck, now we are going on a bullshit story of a picture in a gun! He's lying, David. Let's wait for Chad."

"Nope, nope. Could be true. Galverson was a fucked-up old man," David said. "Could be something he would do." He walked over to Milt, reached into his back pocket, and took out the ripped sketch. He grabbed Milt by the hair and pulled his head up. "You're saying this is where the gold is! This fucking pencil sketch! There's a million shafts out there cut into the rock! How would I find this one?"

"The sketch. Look closely!" Milt said, swallowing hard. "It has a pine tree growing out of the rock at an angle beside the shaft, and one side of the shaft has a notch cut out. Like somebody made a mistake. You would recognize it!"

David let go of Milt's head and walked over to the boys. He leaned over and looked them in the eyes. "Now, what do you think I should do, boys? Should I believe your old man? Or should I shoot one of you to make sure?" He turned around, not waiting for an answer.

"Untie him, Marty, and then tie his hands. We're taking a little hike to the Davidson Mine!"

Marty looked at his brother with surprise. "You're believing this shit, David? Why can't we wait for Chad?"

David looked at his watch. "It's getting close to three o'clock already. Maybe he's lying, but then again, maybe there is no map, and Chad is still looking." He turned to Milt as Marty untied him from the chair and then secured his hands again behind his back with rope. "Besides, if we don't find it, there are lots of places to have an accident while looking!" he said, smiling.

## Chapter Twenty-Eight

# F**CKING MS

Singh and Marsh walked to within fifty feet of the cabin and squatted down. Each was carrying a twelve-gauge shotgun.

"Okay, Marsh, we're going to go straight up to the front door and see if we can at least get a look through those side windows to see what we are dealing with," Singh said, staring straight ahead. He turned to Marsh. "Marsh! You with me?"

"Yeah, sorry, I'm here, sir," Marsh replied. "Sir?"

"Yeah?"

"You ever have to do any of this sort of thing down south?"

"We did enough. Just didn't have to walk so fucking far! Let's go!"

Singh and Marsh came up on the front porch and split up, one going to each window on either side of the door.

They looked in to see Nathan and John now bound back to back in the chairs and Marty DeMello, his back towards them, stirring a pot on the wood stove. They could see two rifles lying against the wall near the stove.

Singh motioned Marsh to move to the door.

"I will go in first," he whispered. "I'm pretty sure that's Marty in there, but I'll get a better look when he turns around. Cover my back and be ready!"

"Got it," Marsh replied.

Singh slowly pressed the door latch until he heard it click. He swung open the door. "Police, DeMello! Get down! Get down!"

He pointed his shotgun at Marty and moved to the right of the table in the cabin.

Marty spun around, hitting the hot pot of canned stew off the stove. He went to reach for his rifle.

"Don't do it, Marty! Get down on the floor, and you won't get hurt!"

Marty recognized Singh. He stood up. "Hey, you scared me, Singh!" he said, putting his hands up.

"Get down on the floor, Marty."

"Sure thing."

"Put some handcuffs on him, Marsh," Singh said as he looked over at Nathan and John. "You boys okay?"

"We are okay," John said, "But it's my dad!"

"Where is he?" Singh said, keeping the shotgun pointed at Marty.

"His brother took him out to the Davidson Mine to find the gold!" John said.

Singh looked back at Marsh. "You got him cuffed?"

"He's cuffed!" Marsh said, lifting Marty up to his feet.

"Put him in the rocking chair!" Singh went over to untie the boys.

"What were you saying? Your dad is with David DeMello?" he asked as he untied Nathan and John.

The boys got up, rubbing their wrists.

"They left about ten minutes ago," said John. "My dad has a sketch of where the gold is. He wants my dad to show him where it is at the Davidson Mine! He might kill him!"

Singh took the untied rope from the boys and threw it to Marsh. "Tie him up on that rocking chair. Give him a taste of his own medicine. I'm going to go after them." He turned to Nathan and John. "You stay here with Constable Marsh. You'll be safe now. I will go find your dad!"

*\*\**

Oakey took his four-wheeler as far as he could before the trail became too thick to drive. He turned off the quad and hopped to the ground. He took his gun pouch off his back and removed the .306 rifle. He could see the Davidson Mine head frame rising above the trees. He took a rag and wiped the gun clean, including Rick's nameplate on the back of the stock. He slung the rifle over his shoulder and started the hike to the mine.

***

Milt walked through the bush with his hands tied, ten feet ahead of David DeMello. He stopped and looked up at the trees. "Starting to rain again," he said. "Mind putting up my hood?"

"Keep going!" David said as he came up and pushed Milt forward to walk.

"What are you going to do with the gold when you find it anyway?" Milt asked. "This all for Fritz Rinestein?"

"Shut up, Tonkin. What do you know about Fritz Rinestein other than your friend stealing and crashing his fucking plane!"

"I know he was with you when Randy Biggs disappeared," Milt said. "And I know he was doing more than transporting gold with his planes before Rick crashed one."

DeMello laughed. "Nice try, Tonkin." He slowed for a moment to allow Milt to get over a log, and then he followed. "You see, Tonkin, this is why people like you in this small town never make it. You have small minds with small ideas. Fritz is someone with a big mind and big ideas!"

"So, this is one of his big ideas?" Milt said. "To get you and your brother to find the gold and do what? So he can take it to Mexico himself and you go to jail!"

"Nobody's going to jail, Tonkin. Told you. Fritz is always thinking about the big picture. He doesn't want to be the criminal and steal the gold. He wants to be the good guy and find it! He tells the Stinson Mine where it is and gets the reward money, but better than that, he becomes the hero. Gets his reputation back."

"You mean his A7."

"His A what? What the hell are you talking about, Tonkin?"

"Nothing," Milt said as he realized even the twins were unaware of the reach of Fritz's drug empire.

He recalled Corbinsky's words about the gold being a drop in the bucket compared to the drug-smuggling operations. "So, Biggs disappeared because he was bad for the big picture, bad for business!"

"Now you are starting to understand," David replied.

"Biggs was supposed to recruit your friend there to sell drugs. Almost did it, too! He just didn't think he would steal a whole fucking plane."

Milt stopped and looked back at David. "Rick was selling drugs?"

David caught up to face Milt. "Was supposed to. He was ready to do just about anything for his mom. We knew that the night way back when we talked to you guys at the NearNorth. Why do you think Fritz sent Biggs after him?"

"Rick was a good person," Milt said as he started walking again. "Even if he did make some bad decisions."

"I would think Fritz and the Stinson Mine would beg to differ."

The two men came to a small stream. "Jump, Tonkin. And don't hit your head again."

Milt made a vain attempt to jump across the small stream, but he fell face down on the opposite side. David DeMello laughed as he crossed by stepping on a rock. He picked Milt up by his arms and looked at his face. "Looks good on you, Tonkin. Now we can't see any blood." He threw Milt forward.

"Let me ask you something," Milt said as he spit out mud. "Trent Campbell."

"What about him?"

"The air tights. Why him?"

"Campbell, he's just a small-time crook. As far as I know, he has been stealing from Rennet for years to line his own pocket. Overheard him talking about wanting some fucking expensive wheelchair for his crippled son at a hockey game last year but he had no money. Let's just say we gave him another option with the air tights."

"How many did he steal for you?" Milt asked, talking over his shoulder as he walked.

"What do you care? What the fuck does it matter? He must have been doing something else on the side anyway, because I heard they delivered a wheelchair to the house last week, and he said he was fucking done with us."

"Really...last week...just like that," Milt said with a smile.

"Yup, just like that. He's just a lucky prick. And you know why he never got fired for all his stealing at Rennet? Because of your union rep there. Danny fucking honest Henry. He would never take anything from Fritz, but he would put his ass on the line every time for you union guys. He told Fritz one time he was principled. What the fuck does that mean? Who would put that kind of bullshit before making a buck?"

"I think it means he had a job to do. Even for someone like Campbell. There are honest people in Tear Falls, DeMello, even if you and Fritz tend to think otherwise."

"Yeah, well, you can throw our new police sergeant in there with him. Not like the old days when they knew what was in their best interest." David took off the canteen hanging around his neck. "Take a knee, Tonkin. I need a drink."

Milt sat on a fallen, moss-covered log while David leaned up against a tree. David looked up at the rain. "You would think we lived in a fucking rainforest."

Milt looked over at David as he drank from his canteen. "What about Galverson?"

"Galverson? You wearing a wire, Tonkin? You're asking a lot of fucking questions about a lot of people."

"No wire. You can check. Wouldn't survive this rain anyway." Milt shrugged as an invitation for David to check him out.

David let out a breath and grinned. "Don't know if a wire is going to be much good to you now anyway."

Milt pressed his question. "You guys kill him? Get rid of him somewhere up here?" He gazed around at the thick bush.

"Now, now, Tonkin. Don't be getting all accusatory over there." David capped his canteen. "Maybe, though, I should be asking you the same question. Because we have no idea where that fucking old recluse disappeared to. He was a stubborn bastard." David scanned the woods. "Maybe he is rotting away up here somewhere with the gold. There are enough shitholes around that he could have fallen down one and no one would ever find him."

David lowered his hood and wiped the rain from his face. "Now, let me ask you a question, Trebek. How come you have never come up here yourself? Get the gold, maybe a nice reward. You knew it was here!"

"My friend was trying to save his mother with that gold, DeMello. He wasn't trying to get rich or pay off another criminal. He was trying to use it for some good."

"There you go with that morality shit again. You really think there is that much difference between me and your friend there stealing? This some of that high school crap of the end... If the end is okay, no matter how you get there?"

"You talking about the ends justifying the means? Not even close. I always saw it as wrong when Rick stole the Stinson plane. Always will. It's the way they treated Rick as a person. They never once gave him credit for anything else in his life. And maybe they didn't have to, but I do. That's what friends do, DeMello. They look at you as a whole person, an entire life, no matter how big one mistake might have been."

"So, I guess if you got to know me better, I wouldn't be all that bad of a guy, is that what you are trying to say?" David asked with a laugh.

"You tell me."

David's smile disappeared. "You're an asshole, Tonkin." He placed his canteen back over his shoulder. "Let's go. And by the way, you didn't answer my first fucking question about the gold."

Milt stood up. "I actually think I did. There would be no reason for me to have the gold. And to tell you the truth, up until today, I was one to believe the police would have figured that out, too. But…I guess maybe not this time." Milt looked up at the rain-filled sky and back to DeMello. "So, why don't we quit wasting time and go find your fucking gold."

The two men broke out of the bush into a clearing dotted by small leafed trees and low brush. They could see a small hill to their left and the Davidson Mine head frame towering to the right. Ahead of them was a rock face fifty feet high and over five hundred feet long. Numerous shafts with dark entrances could be seen drilled out along its length. David DeMello slung his rifle on his shoulder and took out the paper to take another look at the sketch, doing his best to shield it from the rain.

"Start using your eyesight, Tonkin, and find me the right shaft."

Milt walked to the center of the clearing to get a better view of as many shafts as he could. He spotted one that resembled Galverson's sketch. "There!" he said as he pointed through the rain. "That's got to be it."

David walked past Milt to take a look. He turned back to Milt. "I don't see no fucking tree growing out of the rock over there, Tonkin!" He took off his rifle and pointed it at Milt. "If this is some bullshit story to buy your boys time, I can think of a lot of trenches to throw your body down…and your boys!"

"There's a notch on it!" Milt said with desperation. "The tree may be gone now!"

David took another look to see a large portion of rock missing from the right side of the entrance of the shaft. He motioned with his rifle for Milt to move forward. "Let's check it out. Walk!"

Milt now knew his time was limited. Even if he was right, he knew DeMello would not take him back to the cabin. He was convinced he would wind up dead, with his body thrown into one of a thousand trenches dug out of the earth or some other shaft drilled straight down. As he walked, he spotted a five-foot sapling. He caught it with his shoulder and pretended to lean over in pain as he bent it back.

David DeMello ran up to him. "Get the fuck going, Tonkin!" David went to hit him in the back with his gun when Milt stepped aside and released the tension in the sapling. It sprang back and whipped across David DeMello's face, opening a gash and causing him to drop his rifle.

"You fucking prick, Tonkin!" David yelled.

Milt ran as David reached for his rifle on the ground. He picked it up and pointed it at Milt. "Stop, Tonkin, or I will bury your fucking body out here!" He fired a shot at Milt and grazed his shoulder. Milt staggered a few steps and fell.

"Fucking bastard!" DeMello said as he walked toward Milt.

Milt lay in the brush, cringing in pain. He waited for David DeMello's face to appear above him with what he thought would be a final shot. Then he heard another voice.

"Put the rifle down, DeMello, or I will blow your back out!" Singh said.

David slowly put his hands up. He dropped the rifle and turned around to see Singh twenty feet away and pointing a shotgun at him.

"You're under arrest, DeMello, for murder and a whole lot of other shit that is going to put you away for a long time!"

Milt could only lie there and listen to the voices of the two men.

"It was an accident, Sarge! We came out here to find some food. Take it easy!"

"Move away from the gun and get on your knees, DeMello! Hands behind your head!"

Milt looked up at the cloud-filled sky as the rain splashed on his face. He waited for what seemed to be an eternity for Singh's voice to confirm he had arrested DeMello.

He flinched as a shotgun blast and multiple pistol shots rang out. "Fuck!" he yelled. "Singh!"

He lay on the ground and wiggled his body a few feet to rest his head against a tree. He looked over to see the blood running from his shoulder. He tried to repeat his call to Singh, but he was too weak. He looked up to see the figure of David DeMello marching toward him in the rain, holding Singh's shotgun, and he heard him chambering a shell. He thought about Kristen waiting for him to return home. Then he thought about Nathan and John back at the cabin and about Rick and his mother's fucking..."

\*\*\*

"...MS!" Oakey said in his deep voice as he looked through the scope and squeezed the trigger on Rick's .306 rifle. The bullet left the gun at nearly three thousand feet per second. It clipped some leaves, and in less than a second, it travelled the six hundred feet from Oakey's vantage point to slam into the back of David DeMello.

\*\*\*

David DeMello stumbled forward, towards Milt, holding his stomach. Blood trickled out of his mouth, and he gasped for air. He fell to his knees, trying to support himself with the shotgun. He looked at Milt with wide open eyes and collapsed.

Milt took some long breaths and heard Oakey's voice calling to him through the rain.

"Milty!" Oakey yelled. "Milty! You okay!"

"I'm okay, Oakey! Check on Singh!"

Moments later, Oakey showed up, standing over Milt with a hobbling Singh beside him.

"I'm okay, Milt," Singh said. "Fell back and hurt my leg when my vest took the bullets." He reached down to Milt. "C'mon, Oakey, let's get him up!" The two men leaned over and helped Milt to his feet.

Oakey took out his hunting knife and cut through the rope binding Milt's wrists and released his hands. Milt winced in pain as he reached up to feel his shoulder wound. He looked over to Singh, who was now kneeling in the rain to examine David DeMello.

"Singh...my boys. Are they okay?" Milt asked.

Singh stood up and looked back at Milt. "They are okay, Milt. Marsh is back at the cabin, guarding them. Marty is cuffed and tied up in a chair. I imagine there is already backup at the cabin by now."

Milt turned to Oakey. "You saved my life, my friend. How will I ever repay you?"

Oakey turned his rifle upside down and wiped the mud off Rick's nameplate on the end of his gun stock. "Someone has made us great friends, Milty. That's enough repayment for me."

Milt nodded in agreement. He looked over at Singh, who was placing his police rain jacket over David DeMello's body.

Singh stood up and walked back over to Milt and Oakey. "Let's go, boys. This is a crime scene, and I think you could use a hospital about now, Milt."

The three men returned to the cabin, where other O.P.P officers had arrived and were already taking Marty DeMello away. Milt ignored the pain in his shoulder and greeted his sons with a hug.

"Marsh is going to take you home in the police car, and Singh is going to take me to the hospital in my truck. We'll pick up your truck later," Milt said. "I love you."

"We love you too, Dad," Nathan and John replied.

"Let's go, Milt," Singh said, looking at the blood on Milt's shoulder.

Milt and Singh headed out the cabin door as Marsh gathered up the boys' packs.

Nathan ran to the door. "Dad! What should we tell Mom when we get back?"

Milt stopped and turned. "Just give her a hug and bring her to the hospital, Nathan. And tell her to bring our benefit plan for the mine counselling program!"

Chapter Twenty-Nine

# TORONTO

Singh drove up to Milt's house and a throng of reporters, satellite trucks, and curious neighbours. He got out of his cruiser, pushed through the crowd, and rang the doorbell. Kristen glanced through the window curtain and opened the door.

"Hi, Kristen," Singh said as he stepped in. He closed the door and turned back to look out the window. "And I thought it was bad over at the station. All this in only three days? Bet it took some of those trucks three days just to get here!"

"Three-ring circus is what we call it," Kristen said. "We've all taken to wearing Rennet Mine earplugs just to ignore them. Go on up, Rujoy. Milt is just reading the paper and watching all the news reports."

"Thanks, Kristen."

Singh walked up four steps and turned right to walk down to Milt's bedroom. He knocked on the door.

"You don't have to knock, boys. I'm not sleeping," Milt said.

Singh poked his head in. "It's me, Milt, Rujoy."

"Oh, hey, Rujoy! Come on in. Have a seat. You must be a sucker for punishment, Sergeant, to come through that mob."

Singh laughed as he sat down. "Yeah, goes with the territory, as they say, Milt. How are you doing?"

"Can't complain for being shot at," Milt said. He reached over with a rolled up newspaper and parted the curtain of his window to look outside. "And this...it will all go away." He took some pillows and propped himself up in his bed. He turned back to Rujoy with a sombre face.

"So, what's the latest?"

"Well, Marty is sitting in a cell down at the station, and Corbinsky arranged for Fritz to be arrested coming off one of his planes at a Southern Ontario airport."

"Chad?"

"Still looking. But we'll find him."

"Go easy on him, Rujoy. Just a young kid running scared. Probably doesn't know the half of it."

"Not to worry, Milt. Every precaution will be taken to bring him back safe and sound."

Singh stood up, walked over to the window, and took another look at the large crowd gathered outside.

"Tear Falls' fifteen minutes of fame for all the wrong reasons," he said. "It's a shame. I think there are just as many people up at Yars Lake looking for the gold again."

"Yeah, I guess that Chris Berts was right in the end after all," Milt said. "That asshole is probably on his way up here as we speak just so he can write a final chapter to his book."

"Wouldn't doubt it," Singh replied. He walked back to the chair, sat down, and rotated his hat in his hands. "Speaking of final chapters, Milt, I guess you have already heard."

"Yeah, but don't blame Marsh, Rujoy. He's a good cop. He's still learning. He was just trying to defend you," Milt replied.

"No, I don't blame him. Timing could have been better, though."

"Just one of those things, Rujoy. When do you leave?"

"Next week, but that was finalized months ago. Long before this crap hit the fan. Transfers are always that way."

"Who's going to replace you? Or is Marsh going to announce that, too?" Milt asked with a smile.

Singh smiled back. "Guy named Sergeant White...Todd White. Met him a few months ago. He will do a good job for Tear Falls, Milt. You will like him."

"Sergeant White, Todd White...nah, I don't think he will fit in around here. At least not as good as the last sergeant," Milt said with a grin.

Singh laughed. He stood up and reached out to shake Milt's hand. "Thanks, Milt. I was just doing my job, but you went above and beyond. This town owes you a lot. I'm sure they will look out for you, your family, and Mrs. Torrison. Your friend Rick would be proud."

"Thanks, Rujoy," Milt replied. "Hey, listen. Come back and visit anytime. Oakey and I will take you fishing up to Yars Lake. You know, there was a reason Galverson built his cabin up there."

"You bet," Singh replied with a smile. He walked to the door and paused. He turned around as Milt placed a tape of John's favourite band, Toronto, into a tape deck beside his bed.

"Milt, what do you think they are going to find up at Yars Lake after all these years? The Stinson Mine going to get their gold back? Give someone a nice reward?"

Milt reached over and pressed stop on the tape deck. He looked at Singh with a contemplative stare. "Sergeant, you know who the Abby Cafe is named after, right? The original owner's lawyer daughter, Abigail?"

"Yeah... That's just local trivia, Milt... So?"

"You should call her sometime if you ever need a lawyer when you move down south. She's great at negotiating deals."

Milt leaned over and pressed play.

Made in the USA
Middletown, DE
15 September 2019